(IN)VALID CIRCUMSTANCES

A Collection of
Dark Tales & Oddities

Howard Hachey

Fluky Fiction

FLUKY FICTION
Newport, ME

(In)Valid Circumstances
Print Edition ISBN: 978-0-9987173-8-8

Published by Fluky Fiction
Copyright © 2021 by Howard Hachey

www.flukyfiction.com

I don't hate people. I just feel better when they aren't around.

-Charles Bukowski

I don't hate people. I just feel better when they aren't around.

-Charles Bukowski

CONTENTS

(IN)VALID CIRCUMSTANCES

A Collection of
Dark Tales & Oddities

DREAM JESUS

"Okay, sir, that brings your total to $53.69," the fresh-faced clerk said to Tom Stills as he began bagging up the numerous bottles and boxes spilled across the checkout counter. Casually, the clerk looked up halfway through his bagging and added, "Havin' trouble sleepin'?"

Normally too personal a question to ask of a stranger, the young clerk was initially hesitant to say anything at all but couldn't help himself. It wasn't every day that someone walked in off the street ten minutes before midnight and bought out the entire shelf of sleeping medication. Liquid gel caps, dark purple syrups and slimes, little dick-shaped suppositories; Tom had 'em all. The clerk quickly gathered from the man's deeply bruised eyes and patchy five o' clock shadow that the answer to his inquisition was a resounding "yes."

Suspicions deepening, he curiously watched Tom fumble his wallet from the deep chasm of his coat pocket with shaky, vein-riddled hands. Crumpled tens and twenties soon fluttered down like moldy crippled birds onto the now bare glass countertop—wings broken and frayed.

At first glance, the clerk had suspected Tom of being another late night tweaker fresh from his ivory tomb. An amphetamine-fueled insectoid coming off a four-day bender, he could imagine the schlubby middle-aged man skittering through the dank alleyways—scouring all the late-night drug stores for enough supplies to do a new cook. Working the closing shift, the young clerk sometimes saw this kind of thing, but not often. Most run-of-the-mill meth heads weren't brazen or dumb enough to buy fifteen boxes of cough medicine at one spot. To do that would raise some serious red flags and possibly jeopardize the mission. The ones who cooked the shit up knew the sacred recipe, and therefore ranked the highest among the bottom feeders. They're the ones who dispatch the little junk-ants to different locations, spreading out the search and absolving themselves of any suspicion.

That's why, when an overly stoic Tom silently approached the counter with a literal arm full of sleeping meds, the clerk wasn't sure what to make of it. Admittingly, he didn't know of any illegal substances that could be cooked up using those types of medications. Not that the young clerk had any real-world experience in the black-market drug manufacturing game. He bought an eighth of Kush every week or so from his second cousin Leon, but that was about the depth of his involvement. It was just as likely that a new high had hit the market, but hadn't become mainstream yet. Some cool new designer drug with scary long-term side effects—ones that turned your bone marrow to fig pudding or flipped your kneecaps inside out. The clerk's growing curiosity shifted to paranoid apprehension. All at once, he suddenly felt uneasy standing behind the empty counter.

"This is too much cash, sir," the clerk said nervously as he leafed through the change, "you're almost sixty bucks over, here." Helpfully, he collected the extra bills and made to hand them back to Tom.

Tom, in return, only stood there, staring blankly at the fistful of money with an expression of brittle indifference. A dead man's contempt. Unsure of how to proceed, the clerk froze and waited for him to respond. "Keep it," Tom finally said, his voice barely heard over the muzak trickling down from hidden overhead speakers. Before the clerk could speak again, Tom grabbed the stuffed plastic shopping bag and quickly left the store.

Alone once again, the young clerk watched Tom go— his stout figure slowly fading into the shadows beyond the glass door front. He almost felt bad about not making a further attempt to give Tom his change back, but quickly got over it. Pockets now lined with a little extra cash, the clerk shrugged away any lingering guilt and went about closing the store. He counted the register, shelved inventory, mopped, then headed home. As soon as he stepped out into the starry city twilight and locked the security gate over the glass storefront, he had forgotten all about poor old Tom Stills. The sad man with the quicksand eyes and loose wallet never got so much as a second thought. There was no way the clerk—or anyone, for that matter—could've known this, but Tom didn't want or need a second thought. In fact, he didn't need much of anything. Not anymore.

Tom Stills was a man on his way out. And a man on his way out doesn't look back for anything.

With ease, Tom's internal compass guided his slow and steady footsteps down the empty sidewalk. His apartment was only three blocks northwest from here, ten or fifteen minutes away on foot. Mentally separating himself from the forward march through the nightshade, Tom took a fresh bottle of pills from the crinkly plastic bag and cracked the seal. Momentarily halting his sluggish stride to tip back the bottle, he vacantly felt the dozens of gel capsules roll down his throat like a handful of pennies down an open sewer grate. Taking a few hard swallows to help them down, he queasily stomached the stubborn pile before tossing the empty bottle to the curb.

One down. Twelve more to go.

He was about two blocks from his apartment when a sub-molecular ripple of numbing euphoria swept through him. At the feeling, a faint smile crept over his hairy lips. The wheels of fate were officially in motion.

It won't be long now, he told himself, inner voice already becoming warbly and unfocused under the siege of invading chemicals. *Soon…soon we'll finally be together…*

Letting the pleasant thought warm his skin like moonshine, Tom continued to walk along the shadow-stained sidewalk. On the move again, he reached down at his side for another bottle of pills. As he did, his free hand became caught in the sticky webbing of the shopping bag. Forcing his way through, Tom viciously grabbed another bottle and tore it from the filmy white placenta. Wildly, he then ripped the cap off with his teeth and funneled them down. The rush was much more immediate this time—warping not only his cellular make-up, but the physical world around him.

At an empty intersection he staggered, slipped on a crushed coffee cup, and fell headfirst into an overflowing trashcan. Resting against the rotten cushion of garbage, he paused a second to wipe the molded strips of lettuce and shredded newspaper out of his hair. Feebly sitting up, head thumping softly against the heavy brick wall to his back, Tom leaned over and reached with severed hands for his bag. After picking himself out of the can and taking a seat on the curb, he opened another bottle. The pills were kicking in much faster than he had anticipated. If he wanted to make it home in time, he'd have to hurry. Not that it really mattered where he slept now. Once he did, he'd finally be free.

Mind trapped in liminal space, Tom forced a thin

dribble of saliva to his mouth as he tipped back yet another bottle. Belly now churning with sleepy goodness, Tom woozily propped himself up off the curb and pushed onward. As he blindly steered his body through the dark fuzziness that softened every wall, corner and cracked streetlight around him, his muddled thoughts turned inward.

As if recalling the faded memories of an unpleasant dream, he fleetingly reminisced on how things had been before her:

Alone.

Overweight.

Depressed.

Unaccomplished.

Balding.

Perpetually broke.

Truly, Tom Stills was the epitome of wasted societal space. He lived each day as if God had leased him the last forty-two years—borrowed time for a wasted soul. The interest rates alone were enough to make him seriously wonder just how long it would take to bleed out if he decided one day to slit both wrists straight to the bone.

But these negative memories didn't last against the lapping waves of the meds steadily coursing through his veins.

And with the rising tide came the glowing image of his one true love.

The night they had met was no different than any other miserable night of Tom's sad, sad life.

Like clockwork, Tom had gotten out of the office around five-thirty. From there he went straight home and vegetated in front of the T.V. while a frozen pizza scabbed over in the oven. He did this every night, hating himself a little more with each extended commercial break. Tom didn't even like watching television anymore, but what else was there to do? No good books or conversation. Not for him, anyway. He couldn't go out and mingle or dance like he used to. God, how he missed dancing. He remembered all the school dances of his youth with a fondness that only time could ferment. Realistically, nothing was stopping him from putting on a nice suit and heading out for the night, but what was the use? He was a dud. Always had been, always would be. At the ripe old age of forty-two, Tom was no closer to finding a girlfriend than he was at cracking the human genome. Dating sites, mailing lists, chat forums and hook-up apps, there was nothing he hadn't tried. Unfortunately, each venture turned up absolutely nothing. Not a single lady out there showed any interest in him. Eventually, Tom had no choice but to accept this ill-fate, grudgingly learning to settle for what he already had, which wasn't much.

His steady job, decent two-bedroom apartment on the lower east side, and the sweet memories of his youth would have to suffice.

But most importantly, he had his dreams.

Tom was special in this way; he didn't experience sleep like a lot of us do. No, Tom was what members of the scientific community at large would refer to as a "lucid dreamer." While most passively experience dreams from the backseat, simply observing and not directly influencing the fragile sequence of events, lucid dreamers take the wheel, steering and manipulating the inner landscape of their projected consciousness. In his dreams, Tom could literally be anything—do anything. His dreams were warm lumps of clay waiting to be shaped by his confident sculptor's hands. He could fly past the entire Milky Way Galaxy in seconds with nothing but the clothes on his back. He could build up and flatten mountains, even entire cities with one concentrated thought or feeling. Nothing here was impenetrable. Rules and places in this malleable universe all coincided to his inner needs and desires. Everything he would ever love was sacred here. Unmovable. The very idea of anything else was unknown to its cortexual inhabitants, all of which were slaves in Tom's hidden microcosmic world. They had no sense of sexual free-will; the concept didn't exist here, considered holy law.

Every night since Tom discovered his nocturnal powers, beautiful women came by the thousands to sleep with him, each one too eager to patiently wait her turn. Riots broke out in the mile-long lines that circled his monolithic palace in the Himalayas over who would please him the most. Here, Tom was the pornstar equivalent of Jesus Christ himself. A literal gift to women everywhere. He had had consensual sex with every beautiful woman in existence from Joan of Arc to Courtney Cox. Mastering every conceivable sex position known to man, he even invented a few more for the Indians to stick in their Karma Sutra. All Tom needed to hack this treasure trove of hidden pleasures was a lot of willful thinking and a comfy pillow to build it all on.

But after nearly twenty years of wild celebrity orgies and barbarian sexual conquests through the solar system, the sad loneliness from the other side started to leak through to the dream realm. Succumbing to the human condition, Tom had begun to grow tired of it all; he longed for something real. Something permanent.

Then, she came.

It was on this seemingly ordinary night that Tom promptly ate his burnt three cheese pizza, watched *American Idol* for as long as his starving brain could stand it, then went to bed; as was tradition. Soon, *his* world filtered through.

In an instant, his metaphysical eyes opened. Completely transformed, he was now a demi-god. And like any flesh and blood deity, Tom was already bored with himself and his billions of worshippers.

Pouting, he sat on one of the warm white beaches of the Galapagos Islands and moodily flicked sand at a passing hermit crab with the tip of his foot. He had flown clear across the vast spread of ocean to be alone. The only inhabitants of these islands were tropical birds, oversized insects and a couple ancient tortoises; none of which gave two shits about Tom's sexual desires. For that, he was thankful. He relished the radiant heat of the artificial sun as he watched the impossibly blue ocean shiver and dance at his feet.

The little hermit crab, shell naturally painted with a sequence of little yellow smiley faces, scuttled faster towards the water, his pincers kicking up brown puffs of dust. In seconds, the tide rolled in. When it left, the crab was gone. Swallowed up. Not sad to see it go, Tom dug his heels deeper into the wet sand and watched the fluffy clouds float listlessly over the water. They looked like smoke signals from down on the shoreline. He then imagined entire forests smoldering under a giant blanket, his millions of lovesick worshippers signaling to him across the way.

Trying to forget them, he wondered if changing the color of the sun or swapping the sky with the ocean would be interesting or not. In an instant, those same fluffy clouds were now pooling up around his ankles, a cold fog that dampened his skin. Beyond the drifting haze, hovering above the horizon, miles of seawater shimmered and rippled against the sun like a million broken mirrors floating to the bottom of an endless chasm of light. Already bored, Tom nodded his head and allowed natural order to return to the land.

Watching the ocean fall back into its planetary crib, he pondered if there was anything left here that he hadn't seen or created. Just then, a voice from over his right shoulder startled him to his feet.

"Hi."

Slowly, without fear, Tom turned to the voice. There, standing not even five feet away, was a naked woman.

She had a slender, tan body like finely blown glass— long auburn hair hanging in loose ringlets down across her perky breasts. The strong ocean breeze caused her delicate pink nipples to harden, poking up through the soft curls of streaming hair. Her body was living art, her aura powerful with magnetic pulses of sexual kinetic energy. Despite the foreign waves, Tom felt all this with passing annoyance. He had seen a million bodies like hers, all perceptually flawless—inside and out. There was nothing special here.

Then, his eyes reached her face. And stopped.

What he saw almost jerked him clear out of sleep, back to The Real. Where a mouth, nose and eyes should've been, was nothing.

She had no face.

To Tom, the sight was utterly breathtaking. Without thinking, he took several sinking steps forward across the hot sand. Mirroring his every move, she also stepped closer. They were like two suns pulling each other into orbit, both magnetic fields crashing against the strain of an unseen vice.

11

Both ends falling inward, collapsing into one. Their long steps across the beach played out in slow unison. Step by step. At an arm's length from each other, they stopped. Tom squinted against the heavy charge of sunlight pounding down on them and looked closely at the vacant canvas standing open at the top of her flesh-covered easel. It was completely bare—smooth. Not a single hair, line or wrinkle tarnished its taut surface.

Just as Tom was about to ask who she was, *what* she was, the sultry voice returned.

"I am yours," a soft song purred to him from the center of everything. Tom froze, stunned, the salty air of the sea drying his eyes and lips. The faceless woman also stood perfectly still, arms resting casually by her slender hips.

Clumsily, Tom found the words. "But…how do you, I mean, where does—"

Her hand, so small and delicate, found his and held it to her left breast.

"I am of you. And you, you are One." Tom watched her hypnotic form as the mouthless words echoed down from the sky, rustling the nearby treetops and whispering below the foaming crash of the current. All the while, not a single twitch or muscle spasmed on her faux-face. Tom was at a loss for words; none of this made any sense. How could she be his creation? He had never seen, or not seen, her before; in his dreams or The Real. Sensing his confusion, the land said:

"I do not judge. I cannot lie."

Suddenly, Tom understood.

Even though he was the "Dream Jesus" of his inner reality, the power had its slight limitations. One, for example, was that the inhabitants of this Locale were almost identical to humans in their inherent moods and actions. Yes, all the women (and some men) in this existence genuinely wanted to fuck him stupid, but that was it. His power on the people began and ended with sex; anything after that wasn't genuine. Of course, women (and men) tried to convince him otherwise, attempting to, in a sense, "con God." Being known as the Lord's significant other could reap many benefits here. The inhabitants of his world knew of power and greed, just as Tom knew of them in The Real.

To be fair, Tom tried earnestly to find his incandescent madame, scouring the artificial landscape in his head and beyond for the perfect soul among the crowd. The one who would love him unconditionally. And, a couple times, he thought he found her, that one special girl who wanted him for more than just sexual release and social stature. But the eyes…they always gave their ulterior greed away. They didn't love him; none of them did. Never would. Tom tried to use his powers to change this, but it was no use. He had never felt true love, so the blueprints weren't there. The schematics had been lost over years of stiff jizz-soaked gym socks and puss-covered bathroom mirrors. Here, he only had its cheap knockoff brand: LUST. Barely a proper substitute for the real thing.

Tom subconsciously made this new specimen, this eraserhead honey with the body of an earthbound angel. Her blueprints must have come from somewhere even deeper down the rabbit hole than where he stood now.

Hand still flat against her soft skin, the steady *thump-thump* of her gentle heart tapping at his palm, dream-Tom was unsure of himself for the first time. Scared shitless by her sheer level of raw beauty—or absence of—he couldn't move, couldn't breathe, without the pressurized bubbles in his head popping off like a champagne truck driving over a bumpy back road.

This...this is real, Tom thought, letting it all sink in. *Finally, I found you...*

Caving to temptation, they embraced, arms wrapped tightly around each other, bodies tall against the fishbowl sea. Upon contact, Tom melted into her, her skin now his own. And, until morning came, they were One. It hurt to separate, waking always did, but it hurt so much more when he was with her. Tom knew that this world was only temporary; she was only temporary. No matter what, he'd have to wake up and leave her. With pain like that, he might as well sit up in bed, grab a potato peeler from the kitchen and start shaving his body like a giant Red Delicious.

So, every night, they met by the ocean. And every morning they were ripped apart by the rising sun. A cleaver of light and fire, chopping them to pieces in front of each

14

other.

It had been a year since then. A year to the very day, in fact.

The old Catholic Cathedral on the corner of 13th and 12th chimed, twelve chimes in all; its echoes jumping from building to building. Tom knew they were meant to be together. And they would be. In time.

And now, that time had come.

Tom could barely make out the entrance to his apartment building as he drunkenly weaved along the deserted sidewalk, his confident stride all but lost. While thinking of her vacant loveliness, he downed three more bottles and crammed a couple of suppositories up his ass. Tom was alone on the street, had been since he left the store. His worries of anyone catching him and alerting the cops before he could cross over were gone.

If they find me, he bravely told himself, *I'll run into the first building I see and drown myself in the toilet. Just watch*

Hurriedly, he washed down more pills with a bottle of bitter blue slime, long tendril strings of it drooling all over his stubbled chin and down the front of his shirt. He didn't need a medical degree to know this much of any medication was lethal. Two bottles probably would have done the job, but Tom had a feeling that whether he slipped into a drug-induced coma or died of an overdose, he would find his way to her. She'd hop out of that rabbit hole once again to help light his way back home.

A beacon.

Zig-zaggedly crossing the street, he suddenly felt his gut lurch; it was at the tipping point. Tom was quickly approaching the physical limits of what his body could handle. Taking deep breaths, slime oozing into his lungs, he did his best to keep it all down. If it didn't absorb into his bloodstream properly, then this would all be for nothing. Some nosey do-gooder would find him schlepped over the curb and probably call an ambulance. This would lead to Tom being resuscitated, evaluated, then committed. He was so close, no time now for any fuck-ups.

But as Tom's foot hit the first step up to the entrance of his apartment, his body revolted. Stomach erupting, a jet stream of ectoplasmic goop sprinkled with the half-digested shells of hundreds of pills jumped from his body and onto the stone steps. Already on the verge of passing out, Tom lost his balance and slipped in his own spew, dropping headfirst onto the middle step's concrete edge. Covered in sticky sludge and bleeding internally from a fatal hairline crack in his skull, Tom laid there in the looming haze of night, completely silent.

He laid there, and he prayed.

Please, God…just let me be with her. I…I swear…I'll never make the ocean fly again…

LETTERS TO NIKKI

9/12/11

Hello

I just want to start out by saying that
Im your BIGGEST FAN. I love everything
you do. Your music videos tv
appearances your perfume and clothing
line even that delicious sparkling wine
you endorse that looks like glittery
Kool-Aid. All of it. I mean that in the
most flattering way possible. Please
dont confuse my compliments for passive
aggressive bullying. Im not one of
those bottom feeders you see in the
comment section of your YouTube videos.
I would never slander your good name
Nikki. NEVER.

Im sure you get a lot of these letters.
Probably thousands every day. But I bet
most of your fans are too lazy to send
you a REAL letter and not some corny DM

on Twitter or Facebook. I acquired an antique Steinbeck typewriter for this very reason. You deserve only the best in life Nikki. Anything else is well beneath your greatness.

Your probably wondering how I got your address and thats totally understandable. It was very hard to find so Im assuming you went to great lengths to keep it secret. Dont worry though your secret is safe with me ;). All I ask in return (this is not a demand I would never blackmail you my Queen) is that maybe you could find the time to see me in person. Possibly dinner? Not necessarily a "date" just a quiet evening enjoying each others company. No strings attached of course. I live on the other side of the city (not the ghetto) I could make it out to your neck of the woods no problem.

Listen I just know we will hit it off. Ive known since the first time I saw you perform on Jimmy Fallon Live. In the interview after your performance you talked about what finding true love meant to you. And when you gave that heartfelt answer I swear you looked right through the tv at me. You ever have that happen? You ever see a total stranger and instantly have a gut feeling about them? Like an inner itch you could never scratch? An overwhelming stroke of intuition that you and that stranger were two kindred souls torn from the same cloth?

Well thats us Nikki. 2 halves of the same spiritual whole.

I dont mean to come on too strong. I just want you to understand how much you mean to me. Once we meet youll understand what I mean.

The return address on the envelope is fake for security reasons. I heard you and that so called "critically acclaimed producer" are rumored to be dating. God I hope thats not true and just nasty gossip. The tabloids should just leave important people like us alone and stop spreading lies. Fuckin parasites. Am I right? But in case the rumors are true I want to keep myself (but more importantly you my love) out of any drama that your "boyfriend" might try to bring to us. Dont worry. Im not mad about him. Not anymore. You didnt know of our gospel yet. Trust me your ignorance will surely be forgiven. Upon reading this I trust you will do the right thing and call it off now that Ive reached out and shown you the truth.

Shit. Im rushing into things again. Sorry Honey Bunch. Just really REALLY excited to have finally found you. My Muse -- My Flame.

I cant say much more right now but we will definitely catch up on everything when we meet for dinner. The things I need to say should be said in person. How does this Friday sound? I saw that your world tour ended last week. Then you tweeted two days ago that you were "Homebound. Ready to chillax." I know you have a couple places (the manor in Miami and the condo in upper New York) but I read once in US Magazine that your favorite place to go after a long tour is right here in the city. Coincidence? I think not.

Ive gone ahead and reserved a table for 2 at that new Gordan Ramsey place on West Boulevard. Took me 2 weeks of constant phone calls but I got us in. Hope 7 pm is convenient enough for you. Ill be the nervous stud with the single white rose and $800 Armani pinstripe suit in the back booth. Thats right. I got us one of the good tables in the back. Past the bar by the VIP lounge. See? Nothing but the finest for my lady.

I know theres a slim chance you wont take this letter seriously and trust me that would be a HUGE mistake. Not just for me -- your biggest fan and bestest friend in the entire universe -- but for you my love.

Please accept this sudden fate for what
it really is; DEVINE INTERVENTION.

                        See you soon

Dezi Derosa

9/15/11

Ok. Ok. Ok.

Just got back from our "date." The fuck
Nikki?? THE FUCKIN FUCK?? I waited for
over 4 hours for you! Had to eat 3 goat
cheese pizzas just to keep our table
that long! I dont even like goat
cheese! What the hell happened????
Didnt you get my letter???? How the
fuck could you stand me up like that
after everything I told you?!?!?

~~Do you want me to come down there and~~
~~chisel your pretty little face off with~~
~~an ice pick and feed it to your toy~~
~~poodles Taco and LeRoy? Is that it?! Do~~
~~you want me to stuff your throat nose~~
~~cunt and asshole with ammonia soaked~~
~~rags then toss you into a vat of~~
~~bleach?!?! IS THAT IT?!?!?! OR SHOULD I~~
~~PEEL THE SKIN OFF YOUR FAKE TITS AND~~
~~EAT THE PULPY INSIDES LIKE TWO BLOODY~~
~~GRAPEFRUITS?!?!?!?!~~

Im sorry babe. Thats not fair of me to

go off like that. I shouldnt be mad at
you. I know theres a good possibility
that He intercepted the first letter
before you could read it. By He I mean
that fuckin 2bit knob twister that
everyone keeps calling your
"boyfriend." A part of me kinda hopes
thats why you didnt show for our date.
Of all the people you should understand
true love when you see it. Is He always
this controlling? Doesnt He know that
your a goddess? Nothing and no one can
tie you down. Not on my watch.

Lucky for us my Poopsywootsykins Im
prepared.

Luckily I used my brain this time and
jotted down your moms place in Detroit
as the return address. That greedy
asshole will never suspect a thing now.
Dont worry. That little secret is also
safe with me my sexy little luvbug.

A Xeroxed copy of my first letter is
also enclosed along with a couple of
polaroids I took of my dick wearing a

cape I made out of some old panties I found in your trash yesterday. Nice huh? Call it extra incentive on your end.

Lets stick to the original plan and meet next Friday. Same time same place. I will start calling the restaurant to make reservations as soon as I mail this. I can barely wait to see your beautiful face in person. But I will wait. For you my darling I will do ANYTHING.

See you Friday. :)

                         Longingly yours
(Yo Main Squeeze)
Dezi D

9/22/11

5 hours Nikki... I waited for 5 MOTHER FUCKIN COCK SHIT HOURS AND YOU NEVER SHOWED!!!!

Do you want to hurt me Nikki? Do you take joy in seeing my hurt? ~~Should I hurt you? Should I take one of your curling irons out of the bathroom drawer and let it get red hot then SHOVE IT UP YOUR FILTHY CUNT while your tied up to that big imported bed? Would it bring me any joy to see that that hairless little peachfish of yours melt into an Arbies quarterpounder with extra horsie sauce and let the dogs go crazy on you!~~

OKOKOKOK. BREATHE. BREAThe. BREAthe. BREathe. BReathe. Breathe.

I held out for as long as I could dear. I really did. I hope all this anger is displaced on you. I realize now that you couldve run into more obstacles (of course I mean *Him*.) My blood literally

fuckin boils thinking about how bad He
is for you. To you. I thought about him
a lot while I waited at the restaurant.
I was actually really revved up about
it when the maitre d refused to bring
me more avocado dip for my third 4
layer nacho platter. How revved up you
might ask? Well I stabbed him in the
right thigh with a salad fork. You
shouldve seen that faggots twitchy frog
face when I popped him too. Hilarious!
He screeched like a little girl with
gum in her hair then pissed his slacks
in front of everybody. Epic! Lucky for
me Mr Whineypisspants melodramatics
created a diversion so I could run out
the back before security got there. I
think its safe to say we probably wont
be eating there any time soon. Oh well.
No sense in sweating the little things
at this point. Right shmoopey?

Enough jokes. Im very worried for you
love. I thought for sure you would be
there tonight to see me. My heart
promised me you would come. This means
that He probably got my letters again

before you could read it. That fuckin
tool! Does he always go through your
personal mail like this? Or did you try
to break it off with him and he wouldnt
accept the facts? Either way talk about
overbearing. I bet he doesnt even let
you leave the house without at least 5
bodyguards and a dildo shaped taser to
ward off rabid fans. No matter. He
could assign you 50 body guards and it
still wouldnt stop our love. That
fuckin coward. I bet he threw both my
letters away before you could read
them. Thats why you didnt come. Hes
probably getting scared now that the
truths out.

Ill have to go the extra mile this time
to make sure this gets to you. I read
in People magazine that you have a 30ft
steel grate fence around your place? I
looked online and found an aerial photo
of it. No barbwire. No problem. Ill be
delivering this ASAP. On the way Ill
stop by the store and pick up a ladder
and some rope. I need to see that this
letter makes it to your front door

because the mail just isnt working out
for us. No big deal though. Just
another minor setback is all. Nothing
to fret about my precious flower.

Enclosed are copies of the previous
letters I sent. Sorry, I dont have to
time to explain everything to you now.

We will go for the same time and day to
meet (next Friday at 7pm). Im a little
strapped for cash at the moment, so
Dennys on South Broadway will have to
do. I know. I know. Its not ideal.
Especially for someone of your
magnificence. But I figure that any old
restaurant will do just as long as we
are together.

Please burn these letters after
reading. I dont want Him getting in the
way again.

XOXO
Big Daddy D

9/29/11

Your fuckin DEAD. D-E-A-D - DEAD. You worthless sack of protoplasmic shit.

You shouldnt have tried to control destiny. If you really loved Nikki you would want to see her happy. Like we all do. She deserves to be happy more than anyone in all of existence! And if you really loved her like everyone says you do then youd already know that. But you just couldnt leave well enough alone. Could you? No. You had to go and sabotage the will of God. You petty insignificant speck of human fuckin garbage! I know its you that keeps intercepting my letters to Nikki. I know your keeping her hostage from me and our secret love. If you didnt know before now you do fucktard - you have made a big BIG mistake.

If you had just accepted that Nikki and I were meant to be together and let us meet you still might have had a chance to live. Ignorant fool.

31

Man you really fucked up.

Dont worry. Ill be sure to make it
quick on your end. You wont ever see me
comin.

                              Sincerely
The True Son

10/1/11

I did it love. You are finally free. *WE*
are finally free.

Im sure youve heard by now but I just
wanted you to know that yes I took him
out for you. Sorry. For *US*.

I heard what all the news stations are
saying. You must be asking yourself how
I managed to pull off such a heroic
feat and still get away to write this.

Well I saw your tweet earlier last
night about how lonely you were.
Something about how He was stuck at the
studio (beautiful job camouflaging that
message for me by the way) working late
on a hot new project. I found a list of
possible locations online and drove
down to the strip. Didnt take me long
to find a flock of his idiot fans
herded outside. Effortlessly I blended
into the crowd. 3 hours later He and
his entourage stepped out onto the
street to get in their stretch limo.

33

The crowd moved with them. Then like a
cheetah I jumped through the weeds of
people and stuck my 6 inch steak knife
right into his face. Thats when the
sheep panicked. His friends tried to
wrestle the knife away from me (they
didnt know it was duct taped to my hand
though) so naturally I defended myself.
Completely within my rights mind you.
Ended up fatally stabbing 3 of them
before they finally let me go. I
stabbed Him in the gut 1 more time for
good measure right before I ran away
too. No one ever said there werent
casualties to love. Right my little
Strudel?

Now I know you need to play that sad
ex-girlfriend card in the public eye
for a little while so no one suspects
anything. I get that. And those inbred
morons in the Press wont suspect a
thing if you keep your story straight.
Youre an amazing actress so I have no
doubt in your ability to fool them all.
I want you to know that I will wait for
you. But we have to play it safe until

the heat dies down. I want us to be able to live together without anyone sticking their noses up at us at the Golden Globe Awards next year.

After my new drone drops this letter off at your place Im gonna take a nice long bath and relax. I think Ive earned it. You know my thoughts will only be of you. My Queen.

I promise that I will try my best to be patient. At least these high powered binoculars will keep us visually close.

A month from today lets meet at your beach house on the coast. Maybe around 5? Ill have dinner waiting for you when you get there. With my metal detector I found the fake rock (technically conch) you keep the spare key under and made my own copies so just come inside. Ill be waiting.

Also, feel free to wear your sexiest string bikini for me. ;)

Forever yours

DD

10/13/11

I was afraid of this… my worst
nightmare. Come to life.

I did as I said. I waited. And while I
waited. I watched over you. Like I said
I would. And what do I get in return
for my services? For my undying love
and loyalty and support??

GODDAMNMOTHERFUCKINASSFISTINGHORSESHIT!
!!!!!!!!!

I saw the interview you did. Everyone
has. Its been cycling on all the major
news networks for a week now. Jesus
Nikki how could you go on live
television and tell the whole world
that Im a crazy stalker???? Are you
seriously gonna pretend we were never a
thing???? Two faced bitch! I know you
gave the cops my name (which you now
know isnt my REAL name) and the
letters. You even said to that reporter
that I deserve to be executed for the
murder of that fuckin hack boyfriend of

yours. Sorry EX boyfriend. You didnt
even mention that two of his friends
survived the attack. Theres an active
manhunt for me as I write this. The ATF
and FBI both released statements
pleading for me to turn myself in. All
because YOU had to go and deny fate.

Silly little bitch.

You know what slut? I was wrong about
you. Youre not a goddess at all.
Nononono. Youre a goddamn IMPOSTER. A
FALSE IDOL. A WORTHLESS PHONY. You only
exist to draw attention away from the
Holy Truth. And now you have the cops
looking for me? Tsktsk Nikki. Thats a
bad little girl. Dont you know?

Trick me once shame on me. Trick me
twice…

NO! NO! You know what? I will give you
ONE more chance. Our love deserves that
much. Meet me like we originally agreed
(11/1/11) but instead of the beach
house I will be coming to see you in

the city. Be home alone. Or else. I mean it. THIS IS YOUR LAST CHANCE.

Do NOT disappoint me.

11/2/11

How can someone so outwardly beautiful
be so fuckin stupid?

I knew you would give the pigs my last
letter. You soulless two timing twat.
Your a hollow shell of a human. A cheap
knockoff. Something only imitating the
genuinely beautiful and extraordinary.
A fuckin dirty rat humanoid replicant.
But really your much worse than that.
Your nothin but moving ash. Less than
zero.

I watched the 24hr live feed on the
news for a while last night. There
mustve been at least 4 news helicopters
and 10 undercover cops circling your
house. I wonder how it got out to the
media that I might be stopping by? Hm?
If it was you that tipped them off then
your even dumber than I thought.

Thats strike 3 Nikki. Youre out.

My new mission in life is to destroy

the impure. Starting with you love. Thank you for the much needed inspiration. Seriously though I wanted us to work out so badly. I really did. Why did you have to let it all fall apart like this? I set everything up so perfectly for us and you dropped the ball. I wonder...did the other side get to you first? Did you ever see what great things we could have done together? I know I did. I saw it all. We were chosen to rule this world as King and Queen. Hand in hand. Fist to fist. But by denying all that should have been you are blatantly mocking the divine.

This is unacceptable Nikki.

I see your headlining a charity benefit for victims of violent crime. The one honoring His memory. I already got my ticket. Front row center. A cool 200 bucks a pop but worth every damn penny. Think your security will be able to spot me? We both know they wont. How could they? Don't bother lookin girlie.

Youll never see me comin.

Yours Truly,
The Second Vessel

SHORTEST STRAW

Tucked behind the wheel of his old station wagon, Bernie Ketchum aimlessly barreled down an isolated back road in rural Central Maine. Hanging limbs of green feathers caught in the beams of his headlights—ancient spruce and pine—lined the long run of twisted track up ahead. Their branches swayed listlessly as he sped by, gently following his steady trek across the relatively barren countryside before drooping back into aired stillness. Dust-laced pavement unraveling silently underneath him, the receding walls of shrubbery soaked in the ruby red glow of the wagon's brake lights before disappearing back into the darkness. Noticing none of this, Bernie nervously twitched with each passing bump in the road—his pudgy fingers feverishly gripping the worn leather of the steering wheel.

Before breaking himself away from the tightening grip to flick on his brights, he quickly noted the time: 1:43 am.

Instantly, Bernie felt a wave of cooling relief wash over him. The mindless droves of semi-conscious, saggy-eyed sheep rushing off to their day jobs wouldn't start for at least a couple hours or so. With both front windows rolled down, allowing the cool morning air to circulate all around him, the sleeping hills were all for him on this humid July morning. He often took these long drives when sleep wouldn't come easy, but as of late had felt compelled to get out of the stuffy little apartment that he was forced to call home. Of all his nightly rituals, driving these desolate back roads was by far his favorite. Pretty much all day, Bernie would sit in his beat-up recliner back at his single room apartment and just veg until the time was right to head out into unknown territory, searching for nothing but inner solace among the dense, rigid woods of Cumberland County.

Except, that wasn't completely true. Bernie was looking for much more than that. A lifelong native, he knew these roads like he knew the back of his own dick. This wasn't just some random drive into uncharted land; he knew every bump and turn along this poorly maintained stretch of interconnecting roadways. For Bernie, driving the night-shaded countryside was the closest thing he had to a real hobby.

Unless you count pulling the bologna pony, of course.

He knew every dilapidated farmhouse and decorative mailbox from the city limits to the 24-hour Irving gas station in Waterville at the end of his journey. The completion of this nightly quest usually rewarded him a two liter of Code Red Mountain Dew and a couple of Firecracker sausages for the ride back. All in all, it was about forty miles round trip—give or take. Intentionally, Bernie chose not to know the precise distance as to keep The Illusion alive. The Illusion being that he, Bernard "Bernie" Ketchum, was the last person on Earth.

I guess you could consider this neurotic fantasy to be a form of elaborate role-playing, but in a much grander sense. When Bernie cruised down these rustic back roads, he didn't simply pretend that humanity was extinct; he BELIEVED it. He saw all the broken-down cars and folded-up barn houses and speculatively thought, *Wow, I wonder how many corpses are buried over there under that brush pile? Would there even be anything left? I bet they packed in there by the dozens, like rats on a ship, to get away from the blast. A lot of good that did, huh?*

Bernie thinks these thoughts and feels good.

Not so much for the countless mass graves, but for the fact that he was all that was left. At these moments of delusional grandeur, his crippling anxiety is all but gone. He feels an electric current of confidence swelling the shriveled glands of his brain—filling them with a false blueprint of inner strength and pride. Fingers still spasming on the wheel, he smoothly rounded a deep turn in the road, feet tingling against the pedals as he accelerated. Head gushing with bubbles of dopamine, his flabby body swayed a little in the driver's seat.

Please don't assume that Bernie *HATES* humanity. It wasn't that he wanted everyone on Earth to die; he just personally couldn't stand to be around other people. The mere sight of another person—any person—caused his anxiety to gradually escalate into fits of crippling psychosis. For as long as he could remember, the nagging, overwhelming sense of distress and abandonment had practically dictated every personal decision in his rather uneventful life. Being subjected to repeated social suicide for years and years on end had finally wore him down to the soft, gooey core of his broken ego. No longer emotionally competent enough to face even the most minor of rejections, Bernie withdrew into himself and became painfully reclusive. Completely withdrawn from any sort of physical interaction, his only meaningful conversations were held online with other shrimp-dicked losers like himself.

No risk, no harm.

While this had set him back a bit in terms of everyday comforts—going to the store, dating, and practically everything else—the all-knowing, all-seeing Internet filled in the gaps. When Bernie was hungry, he used the Pizza Hut app on his phone. When he needed everyday hygiene supplies, those too would be delivered. He even managed to get a cushy job working from home as a software programmer (for which he got his degree—you guessed it— online). The Internet is so omnipotent and wonderful that Bernie had gone nearly eighteen months without having to make a single phone call.

God bless science.

So, like a pillaging racoon or gutter rat, Bernie waited patiently until the wee hours of the morning to go out and live his ultimate fantasy—a world where he was the only thing that wasn't charred to shit. In fact, he alone would be the greatest thing on God's gray Earth.

The new King of Shit.

With the obvious exception of the occasional run-in with deer, he was free to tool up and down these hills playing Road Warrior until the sun warned him of the end to his morbid utopian dream. So rarely did he come across another person or car on these drives that when he climbed the crest of hill that night and saw a group of small lights at the foot below, he almost impulsively slammed on the brakes. Over the years, he had taught himself how to deal with the human interactions that couldn't be avoided. He was no George Clooney—off by about 180 pounds and a whole lot of charm—but he possessed enough vital coping skills to stay out of the nut house. So, when the glaring brake lights of the nearing car shattered his imaginary veil— forcing him to come back to the now—Bernie's social survival reflexes kicked into full gear.

Gently, he applied the brakes and veered left onto the soft shoulder to quietly pass by the scene. He had no intentions of pulling over or interacting with the people up ahead. Even if the circumstances were dire, which they very well might be given the location and time of day, he would keep on driving. Bernie told himself that he wouldn't do any good by getting involved in the situation, anyhow.

You'll only fuck things up worse, that toxic inner voice toxically added, dripping acidic slime of bottomless self-loathing and insecurity between his crusty, wax-clotted ears.

As he slowly passed, he came close enough to accurately view the two smallish compact cars neatly parked on the side of the road—both with their headlights on and driver side doors hanging wide open. Judging by what little he saw, Bernie half suspected that there might have been a minor accident, or maybe just a good Samaritan helping a fellow traveler with a flat tire. Most likely, car number one hit a deer and car number two stopped to assist. This kind of thing happened every single day in Maine—nothing out of the ordinary. Content with that string of logic, he continued to slowly pass the two parked vehicles, easing himself back into a semi-dazed state of apocalyptic pleasures.

Suddenly, as Bernie was almost past the scene, a dark figure became illuminated by the headlights of the two parked cars. Like a giant tomcat, it jumped out from the right-hand shoulder lane and stood tall in the roadway. With his guard down, Bernie was slow to react to the figure sprinting madly towards his passenger side door. Snapping his head at the sound of feet slapping against hard pavement, Bernie turned his head to the right and saw the unfathomable.

Running towards his car in an open arm sprint was a naked white man covered head to toe in what could only be blood. He wore the blood like maroon body paint—except where some of it had dried and flaked off like dead skin to reveal his reflective paleness underneath. Not entirely naked, Bernie noticed that the man was wearing running shoes and a sparkly ankle bracelet. The bracelet—gold finish illuminated by the car's headlights—cast a peculiar twinkle of comic light on the otherwise dully horrific image.

Bernie wasn't sure if any of that counted as clothing, but it certainly wasn't customary dress to the area.

In the naked man's left hand was a hacksaw—just as blood-soaked as his unsheathed body. In his right hand appeared to be a bag containing something of notable weight. It swung like a pendulum against the man's tender thighs as he scrambled wildly across the cracked pavement. But well above all these eccentric traits, one stood out as the most unsettling.

Covering the man's entire head was a cheesy Obama Halloween mask.

The mask too was spotted with blood, giving it a menacing polka dot pattern that was mostly visible on the president's large grand piano style teeth. Bernie was transfixed by this sight for far too long before he finally reacted. Slamming both feet down on the gas, the station wagon's bald back tires spun—screeching and smoking into the dead of night. But as Bernie and the station wagon only seemed to just float in place on the far side of the road, the crazed man closed in.

Just as it looked like Obama was going to dive through the open passenger window and hack Bernie limb from limb, the station wagon's tires finally caught traction and took off, hitting the ground with such force that the ass end fishtailed uncontrollably towards the soft shoulder. Obama somehow foresaw this and threw the mystery bag with all his might. Despite having a hacksaw in his other hand and a poorly constructed mask over his face, the bag sailed gracefully through the open passenger window and struck the steering wheel with a heavy thud. Screaming, Bernie almost lost his cool and swerved into the ditch. Violently jerking the steering wheel to regain control, the wet sack rolled off its perch on the center console and landed in the passenger seat. Like a clip straight out of a B-movie chase scene, Bernie finally straightened out the wagon and sped off.

In his rearview, Obama stood motionless in the roadway and watched the car peel away.

For five whole minutes, Bernie drove far too fast through the hillside. Grinding his teeth with paranoid panic, he frantically checked his rearview every six seconds until he was certain that Obama hadn't jumped into one of those parked cars and given chase. Scared out of his mind and desperately needing to return home, he skidded onto an adjacent road which would hook him back around to Route 2.

Once out of the woods, Bernie sped towards the

halogen glow of the only twenty-four-hour gas station in town. Once there, he noisily slid into a spot behind some overflowing dumpsters, checked his rearview again to make sure no one was around, and proceeded to weep uncontrollably into his meaty hands. Acne-scarred cheeks flaring a blistered scarlet, greasy tears slid down the many crevices and craters of his bloated face between gasping sobs. Breath tortured, thick lines of drool bungeed from his cold-sore-swollen mouth. Completely alone, he allowed himself to cry through his knitted fingers, straining the stringy flow of oozing snot and tears. Not since he was twelve years old had he been this afraid. The only difference: he wasn't being accused of trying to burn down the rec gymnasium. A naked man, or possibly transgender psychopath, with a weird thing for ankle bracelets was running around the back roads of Maine doing...well, Bernie didn't quite know.

You know what he was doing, R-Tard, that pessimistic voice of self-doubt readily said. *You don't think all that blood was his, do you? Come on, man, get real! Are you seriously that stupid? Well, I shouldn't say that; you did just sit there like a dope and let that crazy bastard toss a bag through your window—*

Bernie immediately stopped crying.

In his blind panic to get himself to safety, he had totally forgotten about the wet bag sitting idly in the passenger seat. Like a burlap rock, it hadn't moved once since its almost graceful descent into Bernie's car. Whatever was inside was certainly heavy. Under the sterile halogen lights of the empty gas station parking lot, he could now see that the bag, like the underdressed man, was caked in a splotchy layer of blood. The smell of old pennies assaulted Bernie's nose once the realization hit him, giving the back of his dry throat a metallic tang. Feeling the sudden urge to vomit, he quickly shut his eyes and thought hard about the smell of bleach. A reliable coping strategy since he was just a little kid, the smell of bleach never failed to settle his nerves. Even thinking about its clean and sterile scent seemed to do the trick. While Bernie was a slob, he did always keep a full bottle of bleach under the sink just in case he really needed it for aromatherapy.

No smell known to man is more clean or pure than that of bleach.

After a couple minutes of reminiscing, he was able to calm himself down enough to pace his thoughts. Bracing for the worst, he slowly leaned over and untied the bag.

Inside the wet canvas sack—like a jumbled pile of mixed hamburger meat—were raw pink chunks woven together with thick strands of tangled auburn hair. Around the giant ball of wet yarn sitting inside the open sack were sharp fragments of broken bone and teeth. If Bernie *had* to guess, the bag of entrails was probably fresh and probably not that of a wild animal. Not an educated guess by any means; he had never been one for hunting or fishing. Never short on imagination, it didn't take much more deduction for him to come up with a viable answer to the obvious riddle.

With trembling fingers, he re-closed the bag—being very careful not to spill any of the rancid meat onto his already blood-spotted upholstery. Slowly, he turned towards the driver's seat and numbly slumped back. In all his extensive preparation and planning over the years of how to deal with practically any social interaction, he had never accounted for something like this. Not a very smart man but certainly not brain dead either, Bernie's first logical thought since fleeing for his life was to call the police and try to explain what had happened. He surely wasn't at fault here, was he? Oh sure, he didn't stop at the scene of what could have been an accident, but if he had played good Samaritan, then who knows what might have happened. Worst case scenario: it could be him grinded up into the president's beef taco surprise bag.

It's not a crime to be a gutless coward...is it?

Bernie quickly decided that no, it wasn't, and dipped into his front pocket to retrieve his cellphone.

Oh my God...you have to be the dumbest, most hollow-headed dick-wipe in all of existence, the voice curtly said. *Of course the cops are going to think you had something to do with it! Look at you! Look at all the blood in your car! You have pathetic serial killer wannabe written all over your big fishy face. They'll take one look at you, your weird ass lifestyle, and lack of alibi and immediately assume that you made the whole thing up to avoid getting caught for—*

Wait.

Caught for what, exactly? Bernie didn't know where the meat had come from—who it came from. Maybe his initial assumptions were wrong. Maybe the contents of the bag were far less sinister—possibly from a deer or roadkill. And if that was the case, then what was the crime in question? Certainly not murder, but maybe hunting without a license? And, really, who would miss this pulpy mess? I mean, in a place where cats and dogs leave in the middle of the night and never return, presumably eaten by a hungry black bear or taking up permanent residency in a ditch, you would never suspect that a madman caught it to play amateur doctor. To most, this would be considered another casualty of the night. Sure, the masked man was naked and bloody in the middle of nowhere, but that didn't necessarily mean he was a murderer…did it?

There's a lot of weird shit in these backwoods areas and—out of boredom and necessity—a fuckload of hard drugs.

And the more Bernie thought about it from this angle, he felt safer in assuming the whole incident might have just been a sick prank carried out by crazy Joe So-and-So high on a combination of spice, bath salts, and Mexican Xanax.

Come to think of it, Bernie hadn't seen anybody out there but ol' Joe. Not the driver of the other car, nor a supposed victim. A part of Bernie knew that something must've happened out there; lucky for him, he had the amazing ability of Mental Gymnastics on his side. One of his special talents was convincing himself that he was never at fault in times of overwhelming stress. If there was a hidden way to exclude himself from a tough or trying situation, Bernie was the master at finding it. He quickly deduced that while the incident was disturbing, it did not warrant the attention of the authorities. Besides, someone else would come along and hopefully call it in only to find out that it was just a dumb prank. Let some other sap deal with the inevitable paperwork and police questioning. The very idea of having to meet and talk with suspicious cops for hours on end was enough to make him feel queasy all over again.

And so, the decision was made.

Sure minded, Bernie snatched up the bag out of the passenger seat, popped out of the vehicle, and chucked the sack into the nearby dumpster. Congealed blood staining his fingers, he absentmindedly rubbed his sticky hands on the front of his pants and roughly slid back into the driver's seat.

"Problem solved," he said aloud to himself, his voice hoarse but gratifying in tone.

Still jittery, but all in all immensely relieved, Bernie started up the station wagon. With a superior smirk smeared across his face, he proceeded to drive home with plans of binge watching *My Little Pony: Friendship Is Magic*.

A couple uneventful days later, Bernie was lampin' around

his dirty apartment—just flipping through the TV channels—when suddenly he came upon a breaking story on the local news that sounded all too familiar.

"This just in," the generic reporter said from behind his long desk in a flat, robotic tone, *a local man in Cumberland County was reportedly taking his morning jog early Tuesday morning when he came across a suspicious looking vehicle abandoned on the side of a rural road. Concerned, the man decided to call in the sighting to the police. Once on the scene, police found numerous personal belongings in the woods not far from the vehicle. Among the found items was a purse which contained a Maine state driver's license identifying the owner and assumed driver as twenty-four-year-old Mary Cyr of Hartland. After an exhausting two-hour search of the surrounding wooded area, searchers came across what was identified as the deceased remains of Mary Cyr herself. While a missing person's report has not been officially filed for the brutally slain woman, police are asking that anyone with information of her last contacts and whereabouts to please contact the Maine State Police."*

The boxed image of the orange-faced news anchor switched to a sweeping camera shot of a busy back road. Bernie instantly recognized the rustic scene—now wrapped in fluttering ribbons of yellow police tape—along with the four-door compact sitting dormant in the swaying grass. Men and women in blue—gold stars embroidered on the sleeves of their shirts—briskly walked back and forth across the narrow screen while the anchorman's emotionless narrative droned on.

"According to what local authorities were able to piece together, the murder took place two days prior to the discovery of the vacant vehicle. And while the specifics of the seemingly random attack are still unknown to authorities, soiled clothing and other personal materials were later found at the scene by detectives and are still being analyzed for any trace evidence that might lead them to the killer's identity. When interviewed, detectives did divulge that there were fresh tire tracks belonging to a second vehicle found at the scene, giving police a possible lead as to what the suspect in question might have been driving that night. Based on these tracks, state police are now looking for a mid to late 70s style station wagon with rear wheel drive. At this time, the exact model and make has not yet been officially determined. If you have any information pertaining to this ongoing investigation, please call—"

Glued to his recliner in abstract terror, Bernie breathlessly thumbed at the remote and shut off the blaring TV set. Ignorantly, he had spent the last two days going about his usual doings as if that horrific night had never even happened—just another bad dream. Previously convinced that everything he saw out on the back road had been nothing but a crude prank, he was now unable to do his usual mental somersaults and backflips any longer.

Too little, too late, Bernie now saw that the worst possible scenarios in life are almost always the ones we make for ourselves when trying to dodge responsibility.

This was something he should have learned years ago through trial and error. So close, but no cigar. Had Bernie just done the right thing and called the cops from the get-go, he could have avoided all this extra bullshit that he so gladly piled onto himself.

Smooth move, doughnut puncher. See what leaving the house got you? If you had just stayed here and watched that stupid pony cartoon you love so much, then none of this shit would've happened. It's truly amazing how little effort it takes for you to royally fuck things up. Truly, it's a gift.

Once again, the voice was right. Even though it *was* the voice's strong opinion not to call the police, Bernie knew that if he had just stayed home in the first place then none of this carnage would be placed on his head. What the hell was he supposed to do now? Calling the cops and fessing up was still an option, but there had to be an easier way to unburden himself. This wouldn't be a boring two or three hour chat about what he had seen that night. Instead, Bernie would surely be subjected to days of intense police interrogation. Everyone knew that the cops liked to find their man quick, even if it meant putting the wrong guy in jail to do so. The general public wasn't very tolerable of an incompetent police force, so sometimes a patsy would be conveniently provided thanks to faulty confessions and highly questionable circumstantial evidence. In the end, everyone is happy and justice is served. Except for the wrongfully accused, of course.

Bernie realized that the tire tracks found by detectives would forensically connect him to the murder scene. Honestly, he could see how it might look bad if the connection was ever made. Risking lengthy interrogations and possible jail time, Bernie decided then that he had to tell his side of the story before the benefit of the doubt fell out of his favor. Feeling confident in his sense of false bravery, he grabbed his phone off the crumb covered coffee table and dialed 9-1-1. But, just as his thumb was about to hit **SEND**, that doubtful voice of reason sprang up.

If you want to spend the rest of your life in a cement box with a scummy toilet as your only source of drinking water, then by all means, call the cops and rat yourself out. Face it, kid; no one's gonna believe a single word that comes out of your fat fuckin' mouth. Better to keep this all under wraps and pray that no one comes knockin' at your door.

Finger hovering just centimeters above the lighted phone screen, Bernie paused to seriously contemplate this very real option. Could he really go to jail for what had happened, even if he wasn't directly involved? He did throw away Obama's mystery meat bag, which undoubtedly contained evidence of some kind—was that considered tampering? Maybe aiding and abetting? Bernie wasn't sure. The afternoon following that weird night in the woods, he had gone down to the carwash and completely cleaned the interior of his vehicle. And if any nosey investigator were to get suspicious and look inside for traces of blood, they would find it; Bernie had done a piss-poor job. More so than the blood itself, they would note the attempt to clean (cover) it all up. That was a *BIG* problem.

Walls were beginning to close in on Bernie, and he had

no idea what to do.

Just then, the voice sympathetically added, *Look, I know this looks bad, but as long as no one connects you to the crime scene, I think everything will work out—*

As if on cue, a series of hard-knuckled knocks erupted at the apartment's front door.

When Bernie was sixteen, he was forced by his mother to get a day job during summer vacation from school. A longtime single mother, she worked countless double shifts as a registered nurse at EMM—the county's leading hospital. But, even with all the extra hours and double shifts, she was still not able to make ends meet. The mortgage on their one-story town house was two months overdue and the electricity would be the next thing to go. Although Bernie detested the idea of working, his mother always had the last say. Conveniently, there was a McDonald's restaurant located only three blocks away that had a HELP WANTED sign. Knowing the anti-social butterfly her son was, Bernie's mom went ahead and filled out a resume for him—making sure the wheels of employment were set in motion. Two days later, the dreaded call came, and an interview time had been set up for the next day. Nervously, Bernie paced about his room for the entire night prior worrying about anything and everything that could possibly go wrong.

Ohmanohmanohman…I can't do this. There's too much pressure. What if they don't like me? Or what if they do like me, and I end up doing a bad job and let everyone down? I can't handle that kind of rejection. Oh God…

When the time came to walk the short distance to his morning interview, Bernie's stomach felt like it was full of angry wasps and used syringes. Dressed in his nice tan slacks and collared dress shirt that his mom had lovingly ironed then laid out for him that morning, he briskly walked toward the downtown area ready to get the whole thing over with. With only about a block left between him and the golden arches in the near distance, Bernie's stomach slowly churned and bubbled with growing unease. And just as he was about to step off the curb and cross the road, a sharp pain shot through his abdomen—stopping him in his tracks. One foot still planted on the curb, he clutched his stomach and painfully winced. Having eaten practically nothing in the last sixteen hours, he knew the sharp pains couldn't be an "emergency" and again chalked it up to nerves.

Pushing onward, he managed to lift his other foot off the curb before the pain in his stomach turned into a huge wet mess in the back of his pants. The audible soiling was so loud and sudden that Bernie reflexively glanced over his right shoulder to see what was happening. Filling every seam and stitch, warm, wet pudding ran down his shaking legs. Staring down dumbly at his own warped shadow in disbelief, Bernie stood on the edge of the crowded sidewalk—steeped in shameful silence.

"Mommy," one little boy yelled from behind him, pointing one stubby little finger up at Bernie, "that man crapped 'em! He crapped 'em!" Disgusted, the child's mother glanced at Bernie with utter disdain—as if shitting your pants was contagious—before quickly rushing by with junior in tow. As they passed, she made sure to give a wide berth between herself and the stinky man. The urge to turn tail and run home at that moment was so great for Bernie that he almost caved to the feeling. But, in a rare act of foresight, he knew that jogging with a wet pant-load would only make more of a mess. So, taking squishy little steps, he slowly turned around and walked back home to take a long shower. His mother wasn't happy about him missing the interview, but she also never asked him to find a job again. Probably out of shame, she allowed Bernie to live with her rent free until he was the ripe old age of thirty-two.

Sitting upright now in his filthy recliner, Bernie was reliving this awful moment in all its vivid intensity.

Except now, he wasn't wearing nice tan slacks to catch the mess.

In fact, he wasn't wearing any pants when the knocking on the door frightened him so badly that he sharted himself. The thin layer of underwear he had on tried to catch the soupy mess that flowed out his backside but failed miserably, spilling hot tea all over his seat. The smell—so putrid that Bernie gagged on the rising fumes—forced him to rush off to the sink in the kitchenette. While frantically peeling off the muddy sheath of underwear and trying to clean up his backside with a dirty dish cloth, the knocking at the front door became increasingly more impatient. Not bothering with the puddle of sludge that now sat in his recliner or the slimy brown trail that led from his chair to the sink, he found a pair of old dirty sweatpants hanging off a nearby lamp and shoved himself inside. Trying to ignore the stench of what could only be described as expired cottage cheese being served in a nest of charred pubic hair, Bernie numbly unlatched the lock and opened the front door.

There, standing in the open doorway, was a middle-aged man of average height and build. Draped in a blue overcoat, he held a plain manila folder in his right hand. If the man wasn't a plain clothes cop, then he should've at least played one on television. His freshly shaved face was stern, accented by a set of chiseled cheekbones and perfect square jawline. An amazingly thick salt and pepper mustache—meticulously groomed—anchored the whole image. At any moment Bernie expected the man to reach into his coat for his badge and say, "Freeze, scumbag! You're under arrest!"

Instead, the man offered Bernie a friendly smile and asked, "Mr. Ketchum, I assume?"

"Y-yes," Bernie weakly replied, unable to keep himself from stuttering. "C-can I help you, s-sir?"

"You might," the man smoothly replied while cradling

the thin folder at his side. "Mind if I come in so we can talk a little?"

As the man was saying this, he simultaneously sidestepped past Bernie and entered the apartment. *Only a matter of time now before back-up is called in to help take me downtown for booking. Oh well, guess your time is up.* Bernie pushed the vindictive voice away and followed the man's careful stride into the apartment. Convinced that this was the end, he reluctantly closed the door. The smell had not improved since he washed his ruined underwear out in the sink, but his new guest didn't seem to notice.

Either this man is a trained professional or he has no sense of taste or smell, Bernie thought to himself as he and the man walked into the center of the trash-littered living room.

After a few tense moments of silently surveying the rounded piles of garbage that bordered each wall, the man turned to face Bernie. With that same warm smile from earlier, he evenly asked, "Mr. Ketchum, do you know why I'm here?"

The man's tone wasn't threatening, but in no way was it comforting either. His dull steel blue eyes—cold and absent like spilled mercury—never left Bernie's taut expression no matter how much he wished they would. Sweating profusely, Bernie made a half-assed attempt at picking up bits of garbage here and there just to keep from having to stand against the man's calculating stare.

"Sorry about the mess," Bernie started to say as he

clumsily balled up old food wrappers. "It's usually way cleaner in here, I swear. Can I offer you a—"

"I'll ask one more time…do you know why I'm here?" Less friendly and complacent as before, the man's authoritative tone deepened with each passing syllable that escaped his tightly knitted mouth.

Swallowing hard with an audible dry click in his throat, Bernie harshly whispered, "No... I-I guess I don't."

"I'm here," the man gravely started, occasionally breaking from his stare to glance here and there around the room, "because of that station wagon parked out front. Would that happen to be your station wagon, Mr. Ketchum?"

"Well…technically it's my mom's car. She makes the payments on it, but yeah, I guess it's mine—"

Interjecting before Bernie had a chance to ramble, the man continued, "Would you happen to know why I am interested in your station wagon, Mr. Ketchum?"

This is too much, Bernie thought wearily, knees shaking and tendons tearing. *This guy is just fucking with me until I give him what he wants. He will keep asking me leading questions until I eventually break into a thousand pieces and confess to everything!*

Never failing to intrude, the voice slyly countered, *Then give him what he wants, you autistic moron! Tell him your story and hope to Christ that he feels pity for your pathetic ass. It's your only chance.*

Once again, the voice was 100% right; now was the

time to come clean. If not now, then never.

Taking a deep breath, Bernie collected his thoughts and said, "I think I know why you're here, sir. If you could just give me the chance to explain what happened—"

"I'll tell you why I'm here, Bernard." The man now stood by the front door with his back to Bernie. Reaching out with his free hand, he calmly latched the locks. After barring the only exit out of the apartment, he then turned to hand Bernie the manilla folder. "I'm here because you know something that you aren't telling anyone. Something that you're afraid might get you into a bit of legal trouble. Am I right?"

Stiffened in a bent position towards the floor, Bernie awkwardly straightened back up and fumbled his fingers on the folder. "Y-yes," he replied softly, all the breath stolen from his shriveling lungs, "I s-suppose that's right…"

"Something," the man went on as if he were carrying on a conversation with himself, "that places you smack-dab in the middle of a crime scene. Am I hitting the nail on the head yet, Bern?"

This was all coming to Bernie from very far away. A defense mechanism, he had mentally checked out and was now emotionally comatose with the various dark fantasies of his inevitable prison sentence. All the group showers and lunchtime beatings were flashing through his mind's eye at lightning speed. The folder dangled loosely between his clasped fingers. Not bothering to open it, he instead set it on the coffee table. Wobbly knees no longer able to support his teetering weight, he flopped back down into his recliner.

Barely noticing the leftover sewage still slopping around in his seat, Bernie commenced to throw his head in his hands and cry. For him, there was nothing else left to do.

"I understand your mental anguish, but you have to get why I'm doing this," the man continued, his tone shifting to one of honest sympathy. "I know it isn't your fault, that you're only the victim of the most unfortunate circumstances, but this isn't something that can be avoided." The man casually crossed the room to approach the recliner. Sheepishly, Bernie put out his hands—wrists up. Avoiding an additional resisting arrest charge seemed easy enough.

Instead of feeling the cold embrace of steel shackles around his wrists, Bernie felt a hard, rigid object being placed into his outstretched hands. Through his blurry, tear-stained vision, Bernie held the hard handled object up and tried to make sense of it.

As his eyes cleared, he saw a rusty hacksaw.

Except, it wasn't rust that was flaking along the toothy blade of the saw.

It was dried blood.

Bernie slowly turned the saw in his big stupid hands until the realization smacked him right in the frontal lobe. *Holy shit-balls!* he screamed inside. *This is the same saw I saw Obama with that night out in the boonies!*

Horrified, Bernie spastically dropped the murder weapon on to the floor and quickly tried to stand up. But before he could, the man was there by his side to swiftly push him back in his seat. Getting a double dose of his own fetid waste—technically three, if you count the initial defecation—Bernie flopped back in his chair with a wet *slap* like a pot of oatmeal bubbling on a hot stove.

"Easy now," the man calmly said, one gloved hand resting stiffly on Bernie's slumped shoulder. "Wouldn't do that if I were you."

Mortified, all Bernie was physically and mentally able to do in that moment was sit and absorb any cruel or unusual punishment that the strange visitor had in store for him. The lack of identification and proper handling of an obvious murder weapon were clear signs that this guy was either a shitty cop or much worse. No detective in his right mind would show up to a suspect's house with the murder weapon just chilling in his back pocket. Even Bernie—a slob with no police training or knowhow—knew that wasn't standard protocol.

As if this strong skepticism were wirelessly transmitted, the man smirked. "No, Bernard, I'm not the police, but I'm perfectly capable of restraining you if you try to get up again. I'm almost done here, so just bear with me." The man bent down and rolled up his pant leg as if to straighten his sock or tie his shoe. Instead, Bernie watched as he removed a sparkly gold linked chain from around his hairless ankle.

It's...the anklet, Bernie distantly thought, confusion mounting with each passing second.

The man stood up and walked towards him, dangling the bracelet between his fingers. "Please don't judge me for wearing this faggy thing," the man openly joked as he paced back and forth behind the recliner. "I didn't want to lose it, being completely naked and all, so I figured I would wear it until the deed was done. It belonged to the girl."

Halting his stride, the man looked questioningly at the trail of brown leakage that snaked across the floor and made a hissing sound through his teeth. "I'm no doctor, but man, you need to get some more fiber in your diet, buddy. Or at least stop guzzling soda all goddamn day." Pivoting, the man motioned towards the pile of empty Mountain Dew bottles and cans that were haphazardly stacked in the corner of the room. "You know drinking too much of that shit can make you sterile, right? Well...no harm done here, I guess."

The man roughly chuckled to himself as he dropped the anklet into a miscellaneous pile of old Charleston Chew wrappers and Hot Pocket sleeves by the foot of the recliner. Standing back up, he dusted off his hands in a quick snappy gesture. "There, all done! Well, I best be heading out. It was nice meeting you, Bernard." Without another word, the man then turned and strode towards the front door.

Snapping out of his pussified state, Bernie slammed his fists down on the chair and shouted, "But why? Why are you doing this to me?! I haven't done anything to deserve this!" His normally timid voice was now a screeching siren of panic. Through the hazy air of the now almost chemical hazard level of stench in his apartment, he demanded an answer from his surprise visitor.

Just about to leave, the man stopped at the open door and slowly turned back to face Bernie in his chair. Slowly, an eerie smile spread under the whiskered umbrella of his bushy mustache.

"I'll tell you why, Bern-dawg. I'll tell you exactly why YOU will take the fall for all this." The man's face was grave, but his demented smile grew. "You see, I'm a very important person, Bern-ah-learn, and important people like me make a lot of money. Now, important people with lots of money make lots of donations and erect many park benches. We are revered by all and answer to no one...except the ones who happen to hold bigger bank accounts. Society has its rules, but to every rule there is an exception. That exception being fuck-tons of money.

"What you saw on that night out there in the middle of bum-fuckin-nowhere was not exactly me, but for all intents and purposes, let's just say that, yeah, I was out there with that girl. I'm not proud of it, but if it wasn't her it would've been someone else. I don't want to get into a whole *psychoanalysis* thing with you, but you get my point, right?"

Too obviously rhetorical a question to answer, Bernie said nothing.

"Anywho," he went on, "seeing each other on that night turned out to be a blessing in disguise. Due to your slowness to react, I was able to get your license plate number and give it to some people who could run it. I mean, come on Bern-Bern, I almost got into your car for Christ's sake! I have to admit, I was planning on killing you until this amazing idea popped into my head. Coincidentally enough, it came to me right before I tossed that bitch's head through your window…"

The bag, Bernie internally gasped. *It…it was a head in there? Oh God…I'm gonna puke…*

"Even though the car is in your mother's name, I managed to get your address from the co-signer's agreement. Almost forty and you still need your mother to hold your dick while you pee? So sad."

Intensely, he left the doorway and stepped closer. "Which brings me to why it has to be you. Honestly, Bern, it's because you're not worthy of the pointless, disgusting life that you live. Even this literal dump you live in is too nice for the likes of you. By taking this bullet for me, you will thereby be earning your place among the rest of us. At first, I had second thoughts about this whole frameup plan, but once the private eye that I hired got back to me with the revolting details of your daily life, I just couldn't resist. I'm so confident that a jury will see how many times a day you jack-off to that weird pony fetish porn and not think twice about locking you up for life." The gap between them gradually closed as the man's steps grew smaller and smaller.

"You fit the social standards of a crazed maniac to a T, B-Boy. It's truly amazing that you aren't the one out there hacking people up. But then again, you can't be a spineless shitweasel and a stone-cold killer. It takes some sort of passion—a sense of drive—that I'm fairly convinced you aren't capable of having. It's odd how most people would look at you, covered in your own shit sobbing like a baby, then look at me, and without thinking twice about it, convict *you* of murder solely based on outward appearance and personal interests."

Leaning into the septic fumes hovering about Bernie's face, the man forced his way into Bernie's line of vision. His catatonic stare at the trash-littered floor was soon filled with the leering smile of a mustachioed psychopath.

"Interesting fact: a lot of prolific serial killers tend to be people like me," the man said, still smiling through the haze of stink. "John Wayne Gacy, Ted Bundy, Dennis Rader…these guys got away with their crimes for so long because no one wanted to believe that someone who seemed so normal and had such influence in his community could be capable of such deception. I've learned that in times of desperate resolve, people will always look for the person furthest from themselves to blame. I know firsthand that the judicial system is anything but fair. It's more like a machine on an assembly line—you being the defective product of society, me being the long steel arm of the law programmed to comb out the faulty or undesirable parts. While you're not guilty of murder, you're guilty of careless neglect to the social standards and norms set forth by the good, honest people who preceded you. This is a big no-no, Bernie." The grimaced face then moved out of Bernie's window of sight. A single gloved finger then wagged down at him from one of the disembodied arms floating just out of frame.

"Shame…shame…shame…"

Bernie saw and heard all this through a quilted veil of stupefied shock. It's as if the voice in his head physically manifested itself into the strange man leering down at him with hateful glee. These dissenting words had been cycling in his head for years and years now, so to hear it coming from an external source was bittersweet. Bitter in the sense that now he couldn't deny such accusations as self-hating nonsense, sweet for the simple reason that this meant he wasn't batshit crazy. The voice in his head wasn't a malicious tumor or crossed wire in his brain; it was his buried conscience trying to reach out and save him.

"Ah, dang," the man said in a slightly humorous mood as he checked his wristwatch. "Look at the time. I really gotta be going before the police show up. I have an anonymous tipster calling in your car in approximately five minutes, so I should probably skadaddle. I would advise you not to run, but I can see that probably isn't an option. See-ya later, bro."

"I'll tell them the truth!" Bernie blurted out just as the man was walking out the open doorway. "I'll tell them that you came here and framed me! I don't know your name, but I know the truth about what happened, and that should be enough, right? Right?!"

Pausing, the man slowly turned back toward the open room. Facing Bernie from beyond the threshold, he asked, "I don't know, Bernie… Does a bear shit in the Pope's hat?"

Before Bernie could answer, the man was gone.

The police showed up to the apartment roughly fifteen minutes after the man's exit and found Bernie still in his chair with the front door wide open. He was crying and thrashing around in a semi-delusional state, barely aware of their presence as they cautiously entered the apartment. With the murder weapon laying in plain sight by his feet and Mary's glittery anklet found nearby, police skipped the usual round of questioning and immediately placed Bernie under arrest for murder. Once forensic teams got the go-ahead to search through his apartment, they found blood-stained pants from that night and the manilla folder on the coffee table. Inside were two Polaroid stills.

One was of a dark-haired girl—mouth gagged and eyes bruised—lying unconscious on the ground, her arms tied behind her back with white nylon rope.

The other, featuring that same girl, showed her with her belly ripped wide open and decapitated head placed neatly on her exposed chest.

The girl in those photos was identified as Mary Cyr.

The severed head was found the next day by a bum rummaging for cans in the very same dumpster Bernie had visited the night of the murder. A forensic analysis of the bag had lifted several fingerprints and hair fibers that were quickly matched to Bernie and the interior of his car. For all involved at the D.A.'s office, it was looking to be a slam dunk case.

Bernie never said a word during the entire length of his much-televised trial. All his personal hobbies and activities were divulged in glaring detail to the public. Police even went as far as to let news crews film tours through his apartment, making sure to get shots of all the moldy food and dried-up jizz rags scattered throughout. His court appointed lawyer didn't want the case but had no choice. Everyone knew that defending Bernie would be next to impossible.

The biggest shock came once the actual proceedings began. Sitting in court with his lawyer, who should walk in and sit at the prosecutor's bench but the mustached maniac himself. Apparently, his name was Rex T. Combs, the biggest and most prolific prosecutor the New England judiciary system had to offer. He seldom lost a case and was notorious for his witty and sharp courtroom banter. Bernie's soul shrank at the realization of the odds stacked against him. Sure, he could call out Mr. Combs in court and try to convince the jury that *HE* was in fact the crazed murderer, but why bother? Judging by the crowd of picketers who spat and cursed at him on his way into court, this would be a futile attempt. Clearly, the people had already made up their minds about poor old Bernie. Trial or no trial, the media coverage of all his personal affairs was more than enough to condemn him.

So, Bernie sat through the entire thing—head down, shoulders slumped forward—and didn't breathe a single word. In the end, the jury took only twenty minutes to find him guilty on all charges and sentenced him to life in prison with no possibility of parole.

Once again, Obama had won by a landslide.

Prison wasn't as bad as Bernie had originally imagined it would be. There were certainly dangerous guys who would stab you in the throat with a sharpened toothbrush for looking at them crossways, but there were some redeeming factors as well. Since his incarceration, Bernie had lost a considerable amount of weight because of the forced recreational time and exercise. The exercise part was hard for him at first, but what else was Bernie going to do for twenty-four hours besides sleep? He learned quick that you could either pass the time trying to forget what you had on the outside, or you could sit in a steel box and slowly go insane with boredom. It wasn't like his cell was equipped with a laptop or TV for him to mindlessly pour himself into as he used to. With all this free time to read and socialize with his roommate, Octavio, Bernie had started to see what Rex was talking about back in his apartment. Finally, he saw the underlying connection of individual purpose.

By far, the best part of prison was the job he got appointed once he had proven himself to be a good inmate. Of all the places in the prison that they could have sent him, the kitchen or group counseling ward for example, he lucked out and got a job washing sheets in the downstairs laundry room. For eight hours a day, *every* day, Bernie bleached and cleaned hundreds of soiled sheets and pillows. He no longer felt immeasurable hate like pits of boiling sewage in the back of his gut every time someone bumped into him in the crowded cells or corridors. The Illusion was dead. His once deep dystopian fantasy now dissolved to nothing but a translucent memory of the night that forever changed his life.

Now, folding sheets and neatly sorting them onto wheeled carts for later distribution, he basked in the euphoric aroma of bleached linens and wondered what the cafeteria would be serving for dinner later that evening.

Bernie thinks these thoughts and feels good.

THE PESCI EXPRESS

24... 3 years dropped out of college—milkin Pop's pension;crashin at old buddies' uptown pad—swank—city livin—sticky fingers...Weekly checks [Pop covers the expenses]—drinkndrugs—food—drugsndrink—support [not out of love]—sheer yellow terror that I'll give up and move back home [you can do that, ya know;pretend to understand]...Can't keep a job in a city full of HELP WANTED signs—not sure—praise Alec;good ol' Alec—him and his grandparents: rich old fogies out of South Beach [Florida]—no rent; no worry—

Write?

Metropolis—miserable muggy September heat—behind noon—spider monkey's bush steams in leather stretchpants—Alec flies through the front door—me, fanning my nuts out an open window—sunburnt kitchen cupboards glow Valencia—sonic vibrations of traffic ping invisible dents to my naked body—

Alec yodels— "Dude! Dude! Guess what?! I got some killer news, man!"

"Yeah? Sup, Peanut?"

Unfazed—step to the window—slaps me from his pocket [slippery fakeness]—Ziploc baggy sucks at my cheek—peel it back—a single piece of stained watercolor paper lines the belly—

"Dude… that better be—"

"Yup! That's right, Tater Nuts! You're looking at 100 hits of high-grade LSD. Whooa, Trey! Hands off. This ain't charity, bro." —celluloid cell wilts back to Alec's front pocket— "I'm gonna sell em for $8 a hit. Primus is playing at the Pier tonight, so I know I can move these bad boys in no time. Got a hell of a deal too! Gonna make crazy overhead on this."

"Fuck that, dude. You'll never sell all that before the humidity kills it. How long they been in your pocket for anyway?" *

*Dr.'s Notes: After some research, I've found evidence that excessive heat and moisture does affect the molecular structure of LSD25. I read from various science journals and online case studies that a liquid to paper transfer should be kept somewhere cool and dry. Away from direct sunlight. Not to be touched with bare skin. Even moderate heat and body oils can dissolve the hallucinogenic compounds out of the paper. Granular sugars and candies—sugar cubes, sour patch kids— apparently work best for liquid transfer. *

Atlas shrugged— "Well, what the hell am I supposed to

do, man? We can't eat this entire sheet. We'd turn to sand."

"Alec, dude, just split the sheet in half and only take 50 with you. Leave the other 50 here in the freezer. That way, if you bonk up the ones you got you won't be completely fucked."

"Oooh, right. Just leave you here unsupervised with 50 tabs of acid. Did you think I'd actually fall for that? I'd come home and find you pulling insulation out the walls and shitting on the ceiling."

"Come on, Alec. Front me til I get my check next Friday. You know I'm good for it."

"Alright, alright. I know you won't get off my ass unless I do. You gotta promise me you won't fuck with the rest of this sheet if I leave it in the fridge. Got it? Promise me, Trey. Only take what's yours—that's it."

Promise—boxer briefs and sweaty handshakes—1 box cutter, some rubber skin [extra baggy from the kitchen]— gently remove the sheet from its womb—tiny beads bubble in the corners and upper lip— "Ha! On the fuckin money!" —repeated imagery occupies every available inch of the sheet—sweat;my face is dripping sea water—ghost image smiles;happy—stuck in a square piss stain—

Grinning—100 tiny white faces—a faded Italian caricature…

Joe Pesci.

Air wet enough to drink—my 10 Pescis slip into a second cellophane stomach—split the rest—

"You sure you want that many hits? I know you, Trey, you'll blow through those 10 tabs before Friday and come back begging for more. You're still good for the groceries this week, right?"

"Yeah, yeah. You know I am. Pop's got it covered. And hey, if these are any good I should be set. With Joe Pesci on em, they best be."

"Is that who that is? I thought it was that weird manbaby guy from It's Always Sunny. You know, the midget from Twins... Danny Devito? Either way, my guy stressed that this is seriously heavy shit. Buyer beware."

Alec shucks and showers—smokes a couple bones— through blue walls of smoke, he again cautions—

"Remember, the guy told me to be careful with this shit, so...BE CAREFUL, Trey. I'm serious. I don't want to come back up here and see the entire metro squad trying to talk you off the roof"—remind him who I am—what I was, will be, should be, could be, to be—and left it at that...Alec bounces out the door;time for Beef Ramen and Billy Mays—*

*Dr.'s Notes: Many researchers and experienced users document a need to not over anticipate these hallucinogenic trips prior to actual ingestion. There is overwhelming evidence that preemptive thinking increases the chances of becoming paranoid or anxious while peaking (reaching highest level of toxicity). Preset notions and standards for the inebriated experience seem to only set the user up for a "bad trip." Professionals *warn that a bad trip should be avoided at all costs. Most are not only mentally catastrophic, but physically crippling, if not fatal. The average dose takes anywhere from 20—40 minutes to enter the bloodstream through digestion. Some batches may take a longer or shorter amount of time to activate (metabolisms and potency vary).*

Black screen, warm speakers—RUSH: Signals [a good start]—bag of 10 chills quietly next to its big sister—defrost—knock the cubic strip to the coffee table—

"so...BE CAREFUL" —Alec's ghost lingers— *"just 2 Pescis... take it slow til you know how fasts them wheels'll go..."*

2 tabs—sit back—little dry strips get nice and soggy—suck, swallow, smile...wait...40 minutes down;sober as a Sunday preacher—nothing—8 hits lay on glass at my knees—10pm: 2 more tabs—chew—swallow...11pm: nothing—2 more tabs—wait... 12:30am: nothing...

Shit news;Alec got ripped [scammed – whamboozeled]— "Ah, fuck it!" —chew the tail of 4—swallow—stupidity, humidity, and sweat compromise the night...10 tabs and not a snap?— "Horse cock floppery," I say—oh, whelp—what's 10 duds to 90? [poor ol' Alec]—I kill the lights then hit the can—

Faint soft secondhand tick—slow and rhythmed to the heat—heavy echoes from the next room [worthless sound]—steady—malleable—not hard in veracity;just loud—the soft tap of a wrinkled finger amplified over giant rubber subwoofers—the bathroom door grinds its knuckled hinges—

"Oh fuck oh fuck oh fuck oh fuck oh fuck" —brass doorknob shivers— "guess that shit DOES work" —paper to hand to ass to hand to paper to ass— wipe/wobble/stand—patchy pants shed like dead skin— open door—[boring] shadows loom—hard air sucking:

    ...TUNK! — TAHTUNK! — TAHTUNK! —

Assaultive pressure points of sound stab at me—walls and floors creepy crawl with sifting energy—funneled perpendicular fluid—auras and halos bleach clean sharp corners—this body of string and glue—hot color;radiated tapestries of paddling shapes and oil acrylics—virtual reality folded in 4s—I reach out...

Lights on—the soft loudness stops [no echo, just recycled air hissing]—same old room—wait for what I [don't] know—I kill the lights and I listen;IkillthelightsandIlisten...

Nothing.

Walk—mirror house length of hallway—cool, crisp bed covers caress my cheeks—head buzz honeycomb, ruffling air of the streets—stomach brain grumbles—the back of my eyelids show me cold pepperoni jalapeño pizza in fridge, [second shelf left side]—corpse legs drag me back through the dark—murky mirror image—kitchen/nehctik—

Two steps of melted linoleum [STOP].

A very short man in a red and yellow leisure suit stands at my kitchen sink—hair, greased back against his skull;taller than his face—shiny black margarine devours all light—a single toothpick splinters his [soft] mouth— bobbing backandforthbackandforthbackandforth— scanning water droplets of rusted air—eyes sharp and flinty like the gold rings around his sausage knuckle fingers—two tadpole eggs rotting in the placenta sack of his face…here stands the missing link between midgets and man;tiny people and giants—teeth long and square like mausoleums behind vinegar cracked lips…he snarks, turns—back set— his elbows rest on the [shiny] metal rim of the sink—my voice, "Is…is that…??"

Joe Pesci—or a seriously dedicated look alike—stands at my nehctik sink.

"Juno's, is good" —his echoed words held a molded timbre—hollowed tones of rust gnawing at corn silo sheet metal— "Jus open tha freezah."

I watch his shoulders separate—his flashy suit jitter and crawl—tumor checkerboards of cloth shuffleshift—head, sculpted entirely of hair, doesn't move—millions of tiny black needles push through bright fabric in softball size patches—bent spider legs feeling and reaching and growing and scraping—flexing longer—the checkerboard starts to break…Joe leans at the sink—[stone] teeth grinding the splinter—the mass of wriggling legs pull the suit to strings— feelers stop—each individual pore closes with a sharp POP at retracting needles…Joe's hairy ass and shoulders trigger my stunted thoughts—

"I…ah fuck…"

Joe's skin ripples at [unspoken] syllables—pigment thinner than a ghost—something pulls the front—Joe's [baby] hands clutch the counter—head buoyed under strain—a loud tear rips over Joe's hairy asshole—forced zipper up his spine—someone screams—

"Jew nose," —another voice full of rasp and fuming turpentine teeth— "is good… is reeeeeaal good."

A wet *SNAP!*—loose skin flaps around his body like a burst weather balloon;beneath isn't bone or blood or gristle or shit—under wet carpet skin lies curved contours of humanity—knotted gridwork of shiny mesh tubes and fiberoptic tendons—stitched and woven together in futuristic intricacy—behind sipping rivers of color runs invisible veins and pulsing organs—light busted clouds of powdered smoke plume out in ionic fog…his mesh body cage bottles its digestive dissipation back to nothing—the inner workings of something impossible flows in and of him—

SLAP!—all Joe's skin piles neatly into the shiny sink—l aluminum claw scrapes cold caulking—other sentient fingers run the stillperfect mold of hair floating in dirty dishwater of skin—

"Choo-know… IT'S … GOOD…" —words and heat come from everywhere—sonic explosions gut cupboards and drawers—shattering plates and glasses—his voice slaps my [naked] body backwards to the cold floor—shrieking feedback chases its tail through my ears...I try, but I can't pull the proverbial icepick from my brain—[quickly] I look up—

Pesci's gone.

My head whips the dark—can't find Paperclip Pesci— his suit of skin jiggles and yawns from the sink—perfect hair forever—I tiptoe through broken porcelain and glass— [gotta reverse this regression]—the open refrigerator passes on my right—But...

HE sees me first—

From the back of the freezer—past miles of cauliflower frostbit plans and crystalized starch—a technicolored walrus slaps its tail—*TUNK! TuhTUNK!*—each hard skin to ice echoes the stretch of [white] nothingness in slow recessions of [frozen] air—visible ringlets tumble towards me at each *clap!*—rolling cotton of fog shrouds the beast— blubber ripples and bleeds together like fighting chameleons caught in a lava lamp...the hypnotic sway of its tail...my head rolls deeper in the freezer—waves of cold air sting my eyes;numb my lips— "Crawl!" something says—I scrunch my shoulders and wriggle—baby worm to momma bird— almost in—the fog clears—miles apart, the artificial breeze drifts the walrus's whispered words—

"Nose hood... bruno, tis you? Job go, go to... dim little smoke drops rain around us... bloody nipples stir shrimp fondue. Tube man, get your coat then... chickittycheck out this scroat before you go..."

Werds—poems of toxic alphabet soup fill everything—
soak through every center of mass—[multiple] astral bodies
strain against this verbal curse inside—I see the walrus
mouth the tundra—[act now]—FLASH—running through
snowbanks—shimmery copper-toothed beast watches from
her white rock—*TuhTUNK!*

I run—look down—feet beaten raw; pink stubs of gristle
and toes—over my shoulder the same pink feet trail off into
nowhere—shreds of me, crumbs of me—I am the
bread/the father/the Sun/the holy spirit—no pain
[nopain]—prismed eyes keep sponging the snow—there's
no end—I turn back to the great white rock and ask the
walrus for help—

No one... nowhere...

Endless ink trails of pink feet walk the horizon on either
side of me.

Wake up—white shirts and wet tubing— "Sir, relax,
you're in a hospital" —strapped so tight to this bed [tied up
or tied down?]— "for safety, sir"—theirs and mine—[mine
and yours]—Dr. Hertel says, "You'll probably suffer from
these psychotic episodes for a loooooong time, Trey" —
flashback to the future— "...prolonged separations of
structure and self... your brain is damaged, my boy; reading
and writing will help with stabilization... maybe bring you
back to normal someday...maybe..." —quarter-sized
pockets of sunshine break over endless fields of ice and snow
and cold and wind and cotton and sound and wind and pink

bread crumbs—lapses of lukewarm sanity—written and [re]written by different stages of me—who I was [am] and never [will be]—

Write?

(IN)VALID CIRCUMSTANCES

"Tell me…did you have the dream again last night?" Dr. Carol Ness softly cooed from the other side of the padded steel door. Though only her emerald eyes could be seen glimmering through the tiny 3x9 inch slot, the fevered scratch of a leaded pencil scribbling on notepad freely invaded the tightly closed room beyond. "Be honest, Dax. I'm here to help."

"Y-yes… It's ha-happened ah-again…" Dax stuttered weakly from his darkened corner, shivering hands and feet dirty from weeks of refusing to bathe. But as mentally disheveled as he was, Dax didn't attempt to forge a coherent lie like he sometimes did during these daily interviews. The little fibs he told were just a means of avoiding the inevitable, but Dr. Ness always seemed to know his true intentions. Slowly and methodically, she'd whittle away at his outer shell of stubbornness using only that purring voice and those jeweled eyes of hers. In the end, the good doctor always got what she wanted. Dax learned this cruel truth early on in his indefinite stay at Clear View Psychiatric Facility. At the end of each hour-less day, it didn't matter what he chose to say or not say during these one-on-one meetings. Just so long as he answered her questions truthfully.

Or whatever Dax happened to perceive the truth to be in that very moment.

Once the dry scratching of the good doctor's pencil ceased, like a rodent with graphite teeth gnawing at a petrified chunk of molded drywall—the chalky sound overly abrasive to his sensitive ears—she peered back through the tiny slit in the door at Dax and calmly asked, "I know we've been over this many times already, but could you please describe for me, in as much detail as you can, what you saw—"

From the far righthand corner of his cell, Dax sprang to his feet like a crank activated toy and charged full tilt for the closed door. "Why!?" he squealed, declawed fingers scrapping and pounding at the sturdy steel frame where the padding had worn dangerously thin. "W-why do I have to r-r-relive this buh-bullshit every-fuckin'-day! Haven't we t-talked about this enough?! Huh?! For the love of Ch-Christ, when's it ever going to be enough?!"

Dr. Ness, all too used to Dax's freak outs, let a tolerant sigh escape the thin space between her pink lips before again patiently speaking into the open divider. "You know why, Dax. In order for me to help you, you must come to terms with this recurring vision that's causing all this paranoia. If you don't, then I'm afraid I can't in good conscience recommend you for release when your case file comes up for review next month." Before Dax could further rage at this harsh ultimatum, she quickly added, "Remember, I'm not here to judge or berate anyone. I'm only trying to help you fully comprehend why your mind can't seem to let go of this particular sequence of unwanted images. Understand? Once you overcome this first hurdle of inner self-acknowledgement, then the process of recovery can truly begin."

Dr. Ness gave this same textbook, trustworthy-and-concerned-health-worker speech every time Dax showed any signs of unwilling frustration with her slow process of analysis. It had been six long months since Dax had involuntarily admitted himself to the hospital, but for him it felt like six years had passed. And through all those frantic days and lonesome nights, he proved to be quite the combative patient. And yet, he had the same dream every single night, just to tell it all again the next day.

Having to be completely secluded from the rest of the regular hospital patients, Dax spent every hour of every day caged between the four blank walls of his cell. The only time he wasn't alone in that locked room with the high ceilings was when hospital staff were forced to come in and administer meds. Never less than five men at a time, they would usually gang up on him in the dead of night while he lay in the corner pretending to sleep. Like moving shadows, they'd slip into his room and attack from all sides. Dax never went into the dark willingly, always fighting back against his faceless aggressors—kicking and screaming against their centipede stranglehold around his limbs.

"Stop! You're killing me!" he'd always scream, his own echoing voice mocking him as he struggled for dear life. "Please, I'm not crazy! You gotta let me out! Please!" But the flawlessly smooth faces of the binding centipede's many heads never uttered a single word in response. Instead, the single fang of a hypodermic needle kissed his skin, saying everything that needed to be known.

You're here to stay, the needle seemed to say while slowly vomiting its sedative insides into the freshly popped ventricle, *forever…and ever…and ever…and ever…*

The only real visual to clear the white static of the buttoned padding from his eyes was a dark yellow stain in the far corner where he sometimes pissed, and the small rectangle of a barred window that hung in the top left corner of the high ceiling. And just like the boundless freedoms he used to know when he was still a functioning member of a free society, the tiny window always seemed just out of reach.

If I could just see outside, he often found himself mumbling incoherently while rocking back and forth on his raw heels, the reverberated sound of his own voice sounding off-pitch and strange to the one juxtaposed in his head, *then all this would be slightly bearable. To see the trees, the grass, the snow, the wind…anything but these fuckin' walls…*

That…and her judgmental eyes…

The prolonged weeks of cold isolation were like a steady trickle of water on his already fragile psyche; slow drip-eroding away all the familiar traits and memories he had accumulated over the thirty-some-odd-years of his normal life on the outside.

Until…until that goddamn dream came along and completely ruined it all…

Sensing that her patient was quickly sliding himself down into a bottomless pit of loathsome self-reflection, Dr. Ness cleared her throat and quickly reiterated, "Please, Dax…tell me, what did you see in your dream last night?"

Stale breath whistling from the panic-torn lungs that rattled in his chest, Dax remained stiff against the hard shell of the door for several tense moments before succumbing to the doctor's robotic charm. Defeatedly crossing the short length of floor in his cell, he slumped back down into the far corner and pulled his scrawny knees up to his chest.

"A-alright…" he finally said, greasy length of snow-white hair dangling over his pockmarked face, "b-but this is the l-last time I'm g-g-g-gonna tell it. I s-swear…"

The dream always starts the same.

It's midday and I'm sitting at my desk by the open window, fingers twiddling over the warped keys of my old

Underwood Champion typewriter. I'd cherished this black beauty since my father gifted it to me on my eighteenth birthday nearly twelve years before. And, besides needing a new ribbon and a couple of replacement screws, she had stuck it out with me through thick and thin.

Or should I say, through bad and worse.

As I type, a gentle gust of city wind ruffles the loose pages stacked by my desk. A simple flat rock I found while strolling through the park the day before keeps the pages from fluttering away like scared birds. This rock, oddly smooth and speckled with glittering bands of fossilized light, was admittedly a crude sort of paperweight, but served its purpose. My desk, on the other hand, was literally just two spaced pillars of orange plastic milkcrates—a piece of splintered planking I stole from an unmanned construction site for a semi-flat top.

It's sad, but even in my dreams, I can't escape the trappings of my pathetically mediocre life.

Curved forward at an unnatural angle, my frail spine desperately creaks under the strain of my bobbing head as I write, begging for me to stand up from my chair and straighten myself out. As a self-imposed freelance writer, I often pushed my body to such pointless physical tortures for countless hours on end just to make a little extra cash. It's quite easy to lose yourself in the open page, especially when it's your livelihood. Finally obeying the urgent call, I rose from my chair to move the stagnant blood in my tingling arms and legs. Relishing the muffled popping of my joints as I stretched, I took a moment to bend down and snatch the curled sheet from the mouth of the typewriter.

On its wrinkled face, a single chain of ink smudged words lined the middle of the page.

Behold, the Keeper of Time, the Mother of all Invention. See me as I see you.

Taken aback, I stood over the page and rubbed my beard stubbled chin. Giving my lagging brain time to slowly digest the cryptic sentences, I wondered, *Odd...why the hell would I write something so...lame?*

Most of the writing gigs I got through my longtime agent were your typical, run of the mill pulp magazine page fillers—i.e., corny soap opera-esque love triangles and gritty crime drama stories. But by far the most requested theme I received from those looking for cheap yet engaging writing was sleazy erotica. And man, do I mean *sleazy*. Acts of farmyard bestiality, innocent characters forced to perform incest and rape on each other, these were only some of the more deplorable topics I'd been asked to pen out in my eight years in the freelance business. The acts themselves might have been illegal, but there were no laws saying I couldn't write about them. Hell, I even got a request from the publisher of some weird Sci-Fi rag out of Taiwan one time that simply read:

Beautiful, busty woman has steamy love affair with well-endowed arachnoid monster. Story must contain detailed scenes of anal, oral, and vaginal penetration. Must conclude with graphic description of woman giving painful birth to a million baby spiders. Between 3-5k in length. Filthy but tasteful.

Being of fairly sound mind, I personally never cared much for these types of stories. But, when you're living through each day on two packs of chicken Ramen and city tap water, your moral stance tends to bend a little. Besides, I knew I wasn't doing any real harm by writing this stuff, just fulfilling a need. Regardless, those types of stories always left a bad taste in my mouth when everything was said and done. And, in truth, I wished I didn't have to write about those things, or at least not so much of it. But these vile little stories made me money—cash, something that my personal collection of writings had never done. I quickly came to realize that the cold hard truth was this:

In order for me to live as a writer, I'd have to put my artistic integrity to the side and shovel through some foul shit to make ends meet.

And hey, who knows? There might be a golden kernel of corn waiting for me somewhere deep in that pile...

It's not like I could really complain that much; I made enough from these trashy throwaway stories to live peacefully in a dingy one-bedroom apartment. And, truth be told, I was completely okay with that. In its own weird, dignifying way, I rather liked the idea that so long as I could put words to a page in a way that kept the publishers happy, then I'd be dutifully compensated.

And so, the cycle continued.

My writing became so frequent that the very act had started to seep into my unconscious mind as well. This made the long days and nights by the open window that much longer, stretching and pulling them into one never-ending sequence of (in)valid circumstances.

But, as I stare down at this new line, knowing full well that I'm standing in another one of these mundane dreams, I couldn't help but wonder what the words really meant. And more importantly, why did I write them?

Then, I hear it.

With an inaudible pop, the air of my apartment seems to suddenly tear and flatten with a foreign pressure that squeezes my bones. The fine hairs on my exposed forearms all raise to attention as my eyes quickly look away from the page and out the open window. The pleasant yellow tint of filtered sunshine is gone, now replaced by an ominously rosy overcast that drips deep shadows of hot pink over the surrounding building and streets. Even the passing clouds absorb the strange light as they begin to swirl and pull towards something unseen high up in the sky. I lean farther out the window in hopes of seeing the source but am distracted by the realization that all activity on the street below has completely stopped. Rows and rows of parked cars line the wide streets by the thousands, people standing about in clustered groups—all of them craning their heads to the sky. But when I try to follow their horrified stares, I'm unable to see anything but the side of my apartment building set against the looming dark clouds that now clot the sky. Whatever was emitting the low rumble and penetratingly soft light was somewhere just above my head.

Oh God, please don't let it be a terrorist attack, I thought despairingly. Anyone who's ever lived in any major U.S. city after the World Trade Center attacks has asked themselves this question at least once. Not that I had ever experienced anything so terrible nor ever want to—my curiosity was fully piqued, nonetheless. Pulling myself away from the window, I did something that I wish more than anything that I could take back. Leaving my apartment, I ran to the stairwell and headed straight for the roof.

Immediately upon pushing my way out onto the tarpaper flat at the very top of my building, I saw it. There, hanging in the sky like a giant cookie cutter silhouette of empty blackness, was a hole.

But not just any hole: a keyhole.

Eyes wide and clothes wrinkling at the inertial pull of the statically charged air, I gawk in dumbfounded wonder as a small flock of black birds seem to fly right through the side of the framed hole—magically reappearing on the other side like the voided space wasn't even there. Suddenly, I realize something important. Something profound.

Wait a minute; they aren't flying through that fuckin' thing…they're flying around it!

Like staring at the world's largest Magic Eye painting, I

could now see that the skull shaped hole wasn't a hole at all, but its own self-contained window—a three-dimensional projection that appeared to face you no matter what angle you viewed it from.

Beyond confused, I feverishly wrack my tired brain for an explanation as my eyes refuse to leave the buttery softness of the pinkish skies. "This's g-gottah be some sort of prank," I nervously babbled aloud to myself, forcing my trembling legs to scramble closer to the edge of the building to get a better look at the unwavering shape above, "or a movie prrr-prop or s-some new publicity stunt or…or…"

The speculative words crumbled to pieces as I finally reach the farthest ledge of the rooftop gasping. Closer now, I can see that the keyhole shaped window isn't as depthless as I had previously thought. Like staring through a literal tear in the very fabric of space and time, a loose constellation of roaming planetary bodies lazily floats by the picture-esque opening.

"Holy fuckin' shrimp!" I scream, unable to keep my panicked thoughts bottled up inside any longer. Filling the eye of the keyhole, completely eclipsing the ethereal space beyond, an eyeless face suddenly appeared.

All teeth—formless head rimmed with infinite jagged points of ethereal spikes and edges—the peering entity stared vacantly through the giant keyhole. Trillions of probing arms splintered like the many naked limbs of a winter striped elm, it balanced itself around the inner ridge of the cosmic tear as deep slits around where its mouth should be opened and closed in great flaps and burps. Puffs of toxic green air steamed from the star sized slits and holes, filling the clean air around its head like a mask of twilight fog that swished and swirled the surrounding clouds of Earth's fragile atmosphere.

Without knowing, I then felt it. Reaching out to me on that rooftop, broadcasting its presence with the bullhorn of the gods. Not physically or mentally—but biologically and spiritually. It was as if my entire body blinked in unison to the filtered syllables of the creature's meatless words.

Behold, the Keeper of Time, the Mother of all Invention. See me as I see you.

And, before the utterance of those words that so ominously appeared at my fingertips not even two minutes earlier finally dissipated back through the molded cheesecloth of my self-projected reality—taking my sleeping conscious and fragile mind along with it—a second gutless vibration crumbled all things standing back to dust.

Existence, or whatever you want to call this thing we all share, ceased once and for all.

The Old Ones had finally returned to take back what was rightfully theirs.

"Mmhm, yes. I see…" Dr. Ness continued to jot down notes

for some time before pausing her incessant documentation to say, "There still seems to be some underlying issues with trust that you need to come to terms with. The faceless monster could easily represent your natural unwillingness to see outside of yourself, or possibly some unchecked—"

Suddenly, the good doctor was struck silent when the entire hospital violently shivered.

"It's happening!" Dax gleefully screamed as he jumped up from his corner. "It's coming! It's coming!"

And as he craned his head to the tiny window, he could see clearly the familiar swirl of pink clouds starting to form overhead.

Soon… he thought, hot tears of joy running clean lines in the dirt that smudged his pale face, *soon, it'll all be over with. Once and for all…*

THE ROT

If there's one thing I know, beyond any shadow of a doubt whatsoever, it's this:

Maine has no more ghosts.

I don't mean this in any literal or astrophysical sense—I'm sure there's still plenty of old haunted farmhouses up in the backside of Aroostook County somewhere. A whole lot'ah suicides up that way, mostly potato farmers who worked their fingers and toes to the bone only to watch their crops either burn or drown, depending on the unpredictable weather that season. You'd think a potato, with how goddamn ugly and tough they are, would be able to grow just 'bout damn near anywhere. Well, this is partly true, but with one major exception.

The soil, just like the people who till it, just ain't right no more.

Now, I say this in a strictly cultural sense. That rugged, individualistic drive—the one that drowned many young men out on leaky fishing and trapping boats at open sea, crushed and mangled them while riding lumber down the raging waters of the mighty Kennebec, Penobscot and Androscoggin rivers—is gone. In the battle of Man vs. Land, Land won in the end.

Ah-yuht. It seems the world don't need their kind no more—the rugged outdoorsman, I mean. But to be fair, I think those days were long gone 'fore my father's father was born—possibly even before that. Way of the world, I s'pose, and there ain't much you can do 'bout that. But it's so much more than that, you see? I mean, sure, the changing times affected things 'round here, but it can't be the whole reason. Hard to say exactly when a spirit leaves a land, especially one steeped in so many boot stamped layers and underbrush that you'll never see the real bones beneath.

Up here, the real Maine still lies dormant just below that rocky soil. Or so I used to think.

It's funny; I always hear the same cluster of words when literally anyone is forced to describe this woodsy pocket of AmeriCanada that I've been residing in for all my life. Quiet. Simple. Rustic. Charming. Cheap. The fleet of summer tourists would all certainly agree with that last sentiment. Every damn year, they go batshit crazy for our cozy summer houses and cheap land taxes, as if they all just happened to stumble upon a secret place where no one knows or appreciates the real cost of the land under their feet. And who could blame 'em for thinking such garish things? To them, the trees and moss and ponds seemed endless. Bountiful. Certainly more than 'nough for every tired city slicker in the world to come by and lay down stakes, build their own furnished log cabin and two-car garage, and lazily waste the muggy summer nights away drinking expensive IPAs and listening to the loons talk to each other from across the star-mirrored lake.

But if you ask me, and ya damn-well should, only one word comes to mind when I'm forced to describe Maine.

And that word, for better or worse—depending on who you talk to, is hollow.

Maine is hollow.

Now, I don't just mean the land, mind you, but the people of this land as well. This goes strictly for the ones who grew up here, them and their ancestors that did the same. The ones that pushed themselves up through the rock littered soils, generation after generation, and reached for that unpredictable sun. Those latecomers who move here to retire or escape their problems from elsewhere aren't factored into this because they are bred from entirely different stock, you see. Maine's a good place to run away to; always was and still is. You'd think that it was strictly because of the seclusion from the rest of the country, and you would be half right in assuming that. The other half, even more important than the first, is that most of us locals do a good job of minding our own damn business. And so long as you and yours do the same, you could practically hide in plain sight and never hear a single whisper of your past catch up with you.

Not all of 'em, mind you; I know more than my fair share of hard-working, honest folk. They reign from all corners of this vast state, but that's neither here nor there. Even they, with their foolishly open hearts and trusting gap-toothed smiles, are at risk of catching The Rot.

What's The Rot? Well, it's not easy to explain, especially to a flatlander who don't know nothin' outside of the long lines and expensive wears of city livin', but I'll give it a shot. Besides, the hell else is there to do 'round here?

The best way, I think, to properly explain this is with an old story that my grand-pappi used to tell me when I was no taller than the prickly raspberry bushes that bordered my dooryard growing up. His dad told it to him, who told it to me, and so on.

Anywho, the story goes like this:

Around 1878 or so, a group of French-Canadian lumberjacks had set up camp along the shore of Moosehead Lake in what's known now as the city of Newport. Nowadays, the place is a just a quick stop off I-95 for tourists to stop and take a shit while headin' Northbound. But ain't that like most good things to go 'n turn to shit after a lil while...

Oh, right, Grand-pappi's story.

Within the first couple weeks of those Cannucks settling in for what was supposed to be business as usual in the sparse milling town, the locals from around the lake started to notice that something wasn't right. The group of thirty or so lumberjacks, all bred and born in the Great White North, began to act very strangely around the locals—becoming jumpy and overly excited any time something surprising or unexpected happened. As if in a trance, the lumberjacks would become immediately dazed after such a scare, numbly repeating back any words they heard like a parakeet shot up with sodium pentothal. Of course, the locals at first went wild and pranked the poor lumberjacks for weeks, drawing enjoyment from what they thought were harmless shenanigans. But when one man was startled so badly that he keeled over and died right there on the spot—another bludgeoning his wife to death after another man offhandedly suggested he do so—the fun was no longer there.

Medical professionals from abroad were soon called in.

This case, later coined as being nothing more than a mass symptom of situational delirium, was first described by a fairly well-known neurologist named George Miller Beard. The man was fascinated by unexplained strange behavior and couldn't pass up the chance to witness such oddness when word finally got around of what was going on up in Maine. Later labeled as Jumping Frenchmen Syndrome, the affected loggers eventually moved back to Canada and the whole thing was soon forgotten. To this day, no direct cause for these strange involuntary behaviors was ever found.

But I know what did it. Sure as shit I do.

Yup, it took me damn near seventy-two years to figure it out, but I licked it. Or, at the very least, I think I've got a loose grip on a very plausible explanation.

The Rot.

I know I know, it ain't exactly as scientific sounding as Jumping Frenchmen Syndrome, but it's the one that stuck in my head, so that's what I'm callin' it.

Huh? I said I call it The Rot, open ya damn ears! Listen, if you can think of a better name, bub, I'd sure like to hear it…

STREET FIGHTS ARE LIKE SNOWFLAKES

Street fights are like snowflakes, I sometimes used to say
"You can always tell a fake from the real thing"
A violent ballet—
Hard hail endlessly pummels the weak into sloping piles of
oozing slush
When spilled, no man's blood can resist the freeze
Pupil-less eyes of penny rust soon polka dot the crowd—
[autistic and cold
WHAP!
[the wet crack of calloused skin when mended threading is
torn for the first time since last
The jawless voices cheer, "Worldstar! Worldstar! You just
got knocked the fuck out!"
Slumped, wrecked, slept, rocked; this is what happens to
those that dare touch the crown
The choice is yours, bub—either eat wind or shit teeth
Catch this fade n' kiss the pavement—Hail Mary, full of
grace
No matter what, don't let 'em see you slippin'
Clout is always on the line

NEW FIX

Body floating as he finally came to, Cody Weaver struggled to open his eyes. Thin knuckles digging and pruned fingers scratching numbly at his own face, he fought against the lingering lull of sleep to rub and pick away the rubber cement from his eyelids. Slowly, the drained color of the outside world came flooding back into his tired eyes like a translucent film of negative white light.

It was only then that Cody realized he wasn't lying in the usual springy comfort of his cum and cigarette stained mattress.

Pounding head reeling downward, he confusedly viewed his naked body—form shimmering in tiny, creased waves across his exposed skin. Except, his skin wasn't the same pale cream with curly chestnut hair that he had become so accustomed to seeing in those most private of moments. Instead, his skin appeared to glow with a pinkish hue, bright and shimmering under the sharp glare of the naked lightbulb above the dripping bason in the corner. Set against the clean white porcelain, Cody slowly came to terms with the fact that he had been soaking in his bathroom tub all night, brining himself like a giant white pickle.

The fuckin' tub? Seriously? he groggily thought, moving his sore arms lazily through the tepid coldness of the discolored water. He was surprised to find that his sagging pectoral muscles were sore to the touch, both forearms lined with random patterns of shallow scratches and cuts. Giving form to his jumbled thoughts, he reasoned, *Well…this is a first. How in the Sam-hell did I pass out in the tub and not realize it until just now? I know I didn't get that fucked-up last night…*

The evening prior, Cody wasted no time dipping into his screw-top cylinder of "brain vitamins" after returning home from a long day of work at the sawmill. Cody never went anywhere without his trusty cylinder rattling away in his front pocket—the *tick-tick* of Death's baby teeth always bringing him immediate joy and solitude. From 9-5, Monday through Friday, he chucked moldy old two-by-fours in a ditch down at the yard. Day in, day out, he spat and swore the prime of his life away at that same dreary lumber yard out in the sticks, never once reflecting on what could've been. Naturally, the work didn't pay worth a tin-shit, but Cody—a thirty-four-year-old high school dropout with two DUI's and a pair of bastard children from two different women in the next county over—never had much to begin with. Never one for proper self-maintenance, Cody and the five remaining chompers left rooted in his cancer spotted gums were completely content with his lifestyle of

116

heavy boozing and mental tinkering with whatever drugs he could get his greasy fingers on. Glass, crack, Molly, weed, booze, acid, Percs, Xanis; Cody was only concerned with burning his candle at both ends.

But, as the rot set in and hollowed out his soul, even he had his limits. No needles had ever popped his blotchy skin, though he supposed that was just because he hadn't brought himself to try it yet. In the end, the how didn't really matter. His every waking moment was dedicated to one thing, and one thing only: the systematic numbing of the hard facts he was now a little too old to set himself back on that tried-and-true path up the winding mountainside of life.

Except now—blacked out, naked in a pool of dirty water—Cody appeared to have stumbled clear off the goddamn mountain and into a ditch along with the rest of the dead wood.

Combing his throbbing head for answers, Cody straightened his weak arms and lifted himself sorely from the stagnant water of the tub. Carefully, he stepped out onto the grime crusted linoleum and approached the lonely sink. There, an open bottle of cheap gin waited for him by the rust spotted faucet. Along with it, his open cylinder of pills sat on the opposite side.

Hot or Cold? he joked to himself through the radiating nausea of the persisting hangover.

Needing relief from the sandpaper grit that lined the inside of his scummy mouth, Cody swiped blindly for the

117

open gin bottle and somehow managed to clutch it on the first try. In two big gulps, he downed the clear liquid, thoroughly enjoying the hard, wet punch it held at the back of his throat. But more than anything at that moment, he wished he could go in the kitchen and make himself a fresh cocktail and not have to drink stale, piss warm booze.

"Listen, kid," his grandfather's voice scrubbed like steel wool through the pulsing grey folds of his dehydrated brain, *"cocktails are like tits: one ain't never enough, two's jus' fine, three's too damn many, and four's ah mothahfuckin' pahty!"* Hearing the old man's raspy, two-pack-a-day voice, his every word capped with a phlegm coated wheeze that worsened until the polyps in his lungs finally shut down the whole club, reminded Cody that he was all he had left for family in his life.

The line stops here, ladies. Come get yer ticket and take the ride while you still can!

Chucking the empty gin bottle into the corner of the closed bathroom, Cody allowed the vaporous liquor to properly siphon through his veins. Soon, a cold stillness settled his quaking nerves. Returning to a familiar perception of normal, he took a deep breath inward and planted his pruned hands onto the front lip of the sink. Wearily, he raised his head and looked into the finger-smudged mirror that hung in front of his haggard face. His lips, usually cracked and dry from the elements, were unusually plump and full of color. The color—the same stale red as beet juice—spilled from his mouth and onto his stubbled cheeks. Reflexively, Cody reached across the sink and grabbed the open cylinder. He'd usually start his morning with a bump or two of speed—the ol' tooth of the bear—but due to the raging headache, he needed to go the other way first. Quickly, he settled on downing a few painkillers to wear off the edge. Knocking out a few Perc 20s into the flat palm of his hand, Cody paused to take one last look at himself in the cloudy mirror and dryly mumbled, "Jesus…I can't 'member a fuckin' thing from last night…" Slowly, he brought the pair of pearly white pills to his plump, red lips.

Suddenly, like layers of sand being pushed away to expose the worn surface of a long-forgotten artifact, it all started to come back in full view.

And as the memories of last night started to flood back to him—the once calming effects of the lukewarm gin evaporating under the rising heat of his pounding heart—Cody numbly lowered the pills back down to the sink and turned slowly to face the resting pink water in the bathtub. Breathlessly, he gasped, "Nah…it…it can't be…"

But no matter how hard he tried to push them away, the horrible images remained.

The long night prior, Cody found himself fully entangled in the throes of a semi-lucid, drug-fueled daydream.

In this dream, Cody's body was no longer his own, his consciousness occupying a foreign entity that was not of any human origin. This body was that of a lone wolf—long, lean, and sleek mass hunkering low to the forest floor. Through the scattered moonlight that poked through the netting of overhanging trees, he felt his empty stomach grumble in hunger as his rough paws stepped gracefully through the tangled underbrush. It was an unseasonable warm night, the humidity in the air clinging to his matted hair like an invisible membrane of moisture. Mind now attuned to the secret vibrations of the surrounding night, Cody unknowingly followed the alluring smell that pulled at his elongated snout. Like an unseen tether, the strong scent carried on the subtle breeze led him blindly through the pathless thicket of brush and trees. Soon, his paws felt the cool hardness of pavement. Standing at the other end of a vacant suburban street, was a long row of sleepy cottage homes.

Obediently, he followed the pull at his nose— autonomously crossing the road and disappearing into the shadows on the far side of a house just across the empty street. The sweet, salty smell that continued to assault his sharpened senses was getting stronger with each smooth step. Stopping his stride briefly to lift his snout and sniff eagerly at the passing breeze, Cody continued to move stealthily along the moonlit wall until coming across an open window. Using the stringy muscle in his new hind legs, he hooked his front paws onto the edge of the low hanging windowsill and peeked inside.

Snoring shallowly on the top of a jumbled set of brightly colored bedsheets was a very young boy, no older than seven or eight. Dressed in matching SpongeBob pajamas, the young boy slept unguardedly in the middle of a toy littered room, his pink face completely slack as he snored up at the ceiling. Even from a distance, Cody could practically taste the unrefined salt brining the boy's exposed skin; the tangy allure of untainted innocence causing his jagged mouth to salivate uncontrollably. Shriveled gut rumbling loudly at the sight, he took all of two seconds before scraping his way up and over the windowsill. Slowly, padded feet impossibly quiet on the shag carpeting of the bedroom, his scaly lips retracted—pointed teeth glinting like filed ivory in the naked moonlit spilling in through the open window.

Once at the foot of the tiny bed, Cody could no longer contain the gnawing hunger inside. In one fluent motion, he pounced. Primal instinct carrying his every movement, his sharp teeth pierced through the soft skin of the sleeping child's neck with surprising ease. In moments, the boy awoke, nubby arms and legs thrashing against the soft sheets of the bed. In seconds, Cody's powerful jaws crushed the boy's windpipe, tearing his throat wide open.

Frantic, the boy gurgled and feebly clutched at the ripping force around his throat as his lungs steadily filled with hot spurts of blood. While flogging atop the already gore-soaked sheets, a large toy firetruck fell from the edge of his bed and clanged loudly to the floor. The battery-operated siren on the toy suddenly started screeching through the choked silence of the bedroom as its tiny red lights flashed, painting the dull white walls in a strobe of dripping crimson. Feeling the vital strength being drained, drop by drop, from the dying boy's body, Cody clamped his powerful jaw down again. This time, the tiny bones in the boy's neck gave a subtle succession of muffled pops. Pudgy hands falling listlessly to his sides, the boy's body soon became still, then limp.

Then…nothing.

Just as the dagger-like teeth retracted from the fleshy pulp of the dead boy's mangled throat, the door of the bedroom swung open with a deafening *Bang!*

There, a middle-aged man in striped boxer briefs and a bleach-stained bathrobe stood tall in the open doorway.

"Billy!" the man screamed, large hands gripping the flimsy wood of the doorframe to keep himself from keeling over in disbelief. Opal eyes set wide and hairy legs trembling, he looked down in mesmerized terror at the blood drenched figure that lurched over his now lifeless son and shrilly bellowed, "Hey! The hell you doin' to my boy?! Get offah him!"

Pulling himself away from the still seeping wound at the dead boy's neck, Cody quickly turned from the bedside and leaped clear out the open window. As his four legs carried him back into the safety of the woods, he could hear the angered screams of the man in the striped briefs echo after him into the night. Like twinkling eyes following his panicked run through the paved darkness, the dark windows of the surrounding neighborhood houses illuminated. Soon, the whole neighborhood was up. Mind now calm and belly full of warm spirits, Cody felt a new feeling inside that was impossible to describe with words. No drug he had ever smoked, snorted, huffed, popped, or drank could compare.

This wasn't the usual feeling of numbed fear or blameless regret. No, what Cody felt was a completely new sensation, a powerful mixture of strength and equilibrium that was formerly unknown to him without the poison of pills and alcohol.

This was true solace.

Wide eyed stare reflecting back at him, Cody screamed in his own head, *Oh, sweet baby Jesus…it's blood! That boy's blood is all over me!* Panic rising, he began to hyperventilate when a sudden realization dawned on him. Forced to think back on all the years he wasted chasing the white horse, he then despairingly thought, *Sheit…this is bad. But…is it really that bad?*

Suddenly, he remembered the power he felt after consuming the boy's untainted blood—hot and sweet.

Lifting his bloodshot eyes back up to the dirty mirror above the sink, a wide smile suddenly bloomed across his face. Right away, Cody could see bits of torn flesh wedged between the large gaps in his teeth—detached smile nothing more than a meat-stained reminder of the unspeakable act that he had committed the night prior.

Unperturbed by the sight of his own ghoulish grin, Cody took a couple of deep breaths and calmly flossed the chunks from his teeth. Not bothering to brush, as to save the deliciously tangy taste in his mouth, he then scooped up the cylinder of pills from the sink. Without a second thought, he dumped the whole container into the open toilet at his side and flushed.

"I don't need you no more," he told the small assortment of pills as they spun, one by one, down the drain. "I got's me a new fix now."

After watching the last chalky pearl slide through the depths of swirling blue water then disappear, Cody hummed a little tune to himself and left the bathroom. Despite not taking any drugs upon waking for the first time in a decade, his mind and body were clear and focused. Polished and new. Once in his bedroom down the hall, he closed all the blinds and laid down atop his messy sheets. Pruned hands resting on his narrow chest, he patiently waited for the camouflage of night to come.

Then, and only then, could Cody get another taste of his new fix.

FROM RAGS TO REDEMPTION

A cacophony of shrill sounds and a magnitude of colorful lights flashed all around. To Steven, the whole experience felt like he jumped into a *Pee Wee's Playhouse* episode while high on bad PCP. Eyes *(How many of them? Hundreds? Millions?)* looked upon his naked body with primitive excitement. There was shouting. There was cheering. There was chaos.

Numbly, Steven thought, *How the hell did I get myself into this??*

"Okay, Steven, it's your turn to answer next," Rich Richardson's voice filled the room with its dark cheerfulness. Neck muscles weak, Steven glanced up nervously at the grinning man. He was smiling his best collagen-lipped smile, making sure that it properly outshone his mustard yellow sports coat.

To the far side of Rich a stage crew removed one of the other contestants from their steel harness. A woman—her left eye dripping down her cheek in black gobs, face bubbling like heated wax. *Oh God…I think she might be—*

"Steven?" Again, that falsely cheerful voice beckoned. Although Rich's clean mouth energetically smiled two inches too wide for his leathery, tanned face, his eyes were sharp and menacing. Full of evil and ill-intent.

After several tense seconds of silence, Steven weakly answered, "Yeah, okay…" He was surprised by how unfamiliar and distant his own voice sounded at that moment, his eyes feeling like someone had plucked out his retinas and stretched them out through his asshole. Even without the heavy restraints wrapped around him, Steven would've been way too terrified to move.

Rich Richardson returned with his slightly widened, white picket fence smile. Reading smoothly off the floating teleprompter, he cheerfully said, "Alright, Steven, here is your question… What was the most painful sexual experience you had as a youth? And please, don't skimp on the details."

Instantly, Steven's mouth slackened, eyes hardening in utter shock at the question being asked.

How can they do this to me?! This isn't right!

All Steven wanted was to avoid a lengthy prison sentence for drug smuggling. Those five tiny beakers of pure Muethinol that customs found in his anal cavity got him nothing but a pending divorce and a dirty six-by-eight cell with no toilet seat. To be fair, he had tried like hell to appeal the twenty years that Judge Dickface handed down to him, but nothing ever came of it. As always, Steven's appeal had slipped through the cracks of the faulty justice system—never to see the light of day again. The first time he stepped foot into his new cell, Steven was convinced prison was where he would ultimately die. Death in the saddest way imaginable.

Alone, surrounded by human-shaped monsters.

But, just as the first-year anniversary of his lengthy incarceration was coming up around the corner, his court appointed attorney came waltzing up to his cell one rainy afternoon and offered him a sweet plea deal. Fistful of papers and a portable thumbprint reader in hand, he waited patiently for Steven to make a decision. And like a true sucker, he willingly took the bait. Hook, line, and sinker. In one impulsive move, Steven scanned his whole life away.

Again.

Prison time can have a way of wearing down a man's sense of mistrust for the seemingly innocent. In the joint, everyone around you is suspect because everyone's guilty of one thing or another. Murder. Arson. Tax evasion. Rape. Drug dealing. Regardless of the charge, there isn't a single person inside who doesn't keep a watchful eye on his own back. But at the promise of freedom, that valuable survival skill can fail. In overwhelming excitement, you can forget that even the man hired by the state to protect you can be just as much of a dirty cunt as Redeye Ricky: the only convicted child molester still alive on Steven's old block. Kid-diddlers and shitty public attorneys aside, most felons are viewed as pimples on the ass of an otherwise prospering society. With that said, Steven should have known from the get-to there was never any deal with his name as the beneficiary.

After getting his thumb and retinal scan, Steven was immediately removed from his cell to be showered, shaved, dressed, and groomed. Accompanied by five armed guard robots, all lumbering cyborgs with dead smiles and rickety joints, he was then not-so gently escorted to a white van with blacked-out windows idling just outside the prison gates. Steven had braced himself against the bitter wind cutting through the meshed fencing that surrounded the prison— his skin still wet from the pressure washer. In the big house, everyone called the guard bots by different names, depending on the block. Most of the time they were called Fagatrons or Gaybots because of the lispy, effeminate way they were programmed to talk. The unintentionally funny design was probably to give the Bots a more nonthreatening appearance. The soft voice was pretty funny until you found yourself being cocooned by a swarm of cold coded automatons in the middle of the night. The checkered red glow of their sentient eyes reading every physiological shift of your cellular construction was unsettling, to say the least. Everything from your body temp to your organ functions was recorded for later medical diagnostics. Of course, the inmates still screamed and threw cum, shit, and piss at them as they would with any other type of guard, but ironically,

129

the machines always got the last laugh.

The drone guards couldn't process external stimuli. Or at least, if they could they didn't react to anything that the inmates said to them. You could scream vile threats into their floppy, rubber-nosed faces until your lungs collapsed; it would just stare back at you with the same unblinking coldness of a walking toaster. The guards addressed and commanded the prisoners in gentle electric whispers—a rather alien sound among the constant shouting and slamming that echoed throughout every corridor of the monkey house. Steven later came to compare their eerie bionic tongue to that weird talking spaceship from an old sci-fi movie he saw as a kid.

Kubrick, I think?

Steven and his aluminum entourage rode silently for what felt like hours until the self-driving shuttle randomly stopped. Knowing he wouldn't get an answer, he started to ask where they were taking him when the guard to his left swiveled its generic peach-skinned face towards his. Bent tube exuding from its empty eyes, it proceeded to douse him with some sort of sticky sedative spray. Its hollow eyes exhausted a wisp of purple vapor that slithered its way through the air like a molecular serpent. While Steven thrashed in his seat trying to fight the invading gases, a black hood was shoved over his head from behind. Arms clamped and legs bound, he felt several inhuman hands swiftly pull him out into the stiff coldness of the night. Body being dragged steadily along, Steven's doped mind spiraled into nowhere. No longer able to see where he was going, the vapor provided soothing visuals to overlap the wall of darkness that hung around his eyes.

An unmeasurable amount of time later, he had awoken strapped to an erected podium that sat in the middle of a fully lit sound stage.

"Steven, we're waiting." Rich gestured with one long, sweeping arm to the unseen crowd and cameras just beyond the veil of piercing light that encompassed the stage.

Steven may not have known exactly how he had ended up in this place, but he definitely knew *where* he was. All too late, he realized that he had inadvertently signed himself up for a televised rehab program for soon-to-be released convicts and felons.

I… am an asshole…

Rich Richardson's From Rags to Redemption was on all digital platforms and available everywhere in the known world. It wasn't always like this, though. It wasn't until the inception of WWIII that attitudes and ideas started to change among the common people. And the entire world watched it all go down firsthand. No one wanted global conflict, but here we were. Spending all our money on defense drones and radiation resistant bunkers—everyone was unified in fear. Never getting to truly relax. Five long years of lying awake at night wondering if you would be the next to wake up and find all your loved ones gassed to death by a Russian drone brigade. Well, it wasn't really gas that they used, but a weird neurotoxin that directly infiltrates the nervous center of the brain. Once distributed into the subject's immune system, the toxin destroys white blood cells at an ultra-elevated rate, causing the person to...

Sorry, I digress.

The war, mainly between Russia and China, involved most of the world due to its implications. Russia, being a nuclear superpower, didn't take lightly to the irreverent boasting of Chinese officials after they successfully developed the first self-functioning carbonless plane. Capable of intergalactic space travel, the Tachyon Airship was a huge step forward in luxury travel and space exploration. For only double the price of a regular plane ticket, you could travel to the moon in less than two days. The ship isn't equipped for long-term space travel yet, but that day was not far off. The completely self-powered, energy efficient new airline company made trillions almost overnight. And when China started to overflow with Yuan, its ego and military also grew.

Russia initially started the war. Not officially through public or political channels, but subversively through cyberterrorism and random bombing attacks, all later revealed to have been set up to look like the act of a random radicalized group of Indian arsonists called Nafrat Beej.

Meaning: Hate Seed.

It didn't take the Chinese long to figure out that the

Russians were fucking with them. A lot of words over world news channels were exchanged, but no one ever really thought it would escalate to this point. On November 15, 2028, the first two waves of ballistically-armed militarized drones crossed both borders. To this day, no one really knows which side fired the first shot.

After the initial handful of strikes, other nations got involved, and soon we had ourselves our first World War in a millennium. It was as if some maniacal force was waiting for the turn of the century to force remembrance of real peril and hardship on an over-privileged and ungrateful civilization that was sterilized of it. For the first time in nearly everyone's lives, cold hard reality checked in to say hello. It stayed for two whole years until suddenly we were saved. No, the war wasn't over—not even close. But, don't worry; people had a new and exciting thing to take their minds off of the global crisis. Something that appeared to be new but was actually as old as man.

Animalistic scapegoating.

Find an undesirable social group that loosely aligns with the things wrong with your faulty reality and violently condemn them for it. Blame a crowd for the actions of a few and then get out of there. Let them know what they have done to you. Meet their pleas of mercy with savage hate, for their whining apologies are as empty as their blackened hearts. They know what they did, and in secrecy they laugh at our pain. Why shouldn't you feel good at the expense of subclass suffering?

Which brings us to the birth of *Rich Richardson's From Rags to Redemption.*

Sensing the growing tension around the world, special interest groups acted fast. They quickly devised a plan to soothe the unsettled masses. War at this magnitude is pure gold for the entertainment industry. Now more than ever, engaging entertainment is needed. The powers that be decided it was time to pull out the big guns.

Originally airing in early 2032, *From Rags to Redemption* was met with grave criticism at first by many top humanitarian officials claiming the show to be nothing but *"snuff porn for the ever-growing group of unempathetic degenerates who are set out to destroy wholesome traditional values... Simpletons drawing nothing but pleasure or discontent from the suffering of others."* The ill praise was soon statistically renounced once national violence and crime rates dropped to historically low numbers for the first time in years. The show created the perfect outlet for most people's primal urges and a means of escape for those who felt disenfranchised by the war.

Almost everyone in this modern version of society either actively watched or knew of the show. Even those who didn't agree with the idea of televised killings had little doubt to the correlation between the show and the now utopian paradise that America had always strived to be. It didn't take long for the people to learn that it took fresh blood to grease the rusty wheels of progress. And lots of it. The ancient Romans and Greeks knew this. The British and colonial Americans knew it too. Basically, every nation in the world has at one time or another turned the act of death into public spectacle. It's a humbling tradition that refuses to die. The powerful special interest groups decided then and there that it was time to bring back the old to cope with the new.

Only, this old hat had a few new rabbits waiting inside.

As is tradition, the contestants featured on *From Rags to Redemption* were always presented as just lowlifes playing their way out of prison and trying to win their ticket back to freedom. If the contestant could honestly answer five simple questions, they stood to win a million dollars in cash and a clean rap sheet. The winner could then go on to pursue a placidly normal life without the shameful branding that comes with being a registered felon. Obviously, you could see why this might seem appealing to a lot of guys in the joint.

But here's the part they don't tell you.

The "willing" contestants are hooked up to psychokinetic instruments that read their brainwaves like giant rolodexes. The machine is able to do this—the opening credits always explain in sexy neon print—through two tiny silver hooks that loop into the exposed frontal lobe through a surgically lasered opening at the top of the skull. This means that your brain's grey mass of knotted lumps is left pulsing and juicing in its tiny flesh window for all to see and hear. From this exposed mass, the thought and memory pulses are projected to a huge holographic platform at the front of the stage.

Nonono…I can hear the wires in my ear humming now. They must be starting up the machines…

With Rich's question still hanging in the crowded studio, the curtained silence forced Steven to internalize his angst.

Arms and legs twitching under the tight straps and restraints, he could feel the cool air flowing through the various stage fans and vents tickling at his exposed thoughts. Brain being feathered by the cold, oscillated air, the shriveling sensation left him feeling like a drying sponge. Vision split, Steven could only see what was before him in watery fragments.

The wires spilling out of his cracked skull were hooked up to machines specifically designed to scan the most embarrassing and degrading memories of the past. All gathered information from the precursory scan is uploaded to the teleprompter for Rich Richardson to read out loud in the form of a vague question. If the contestant answered the question correctly with no trace of deception, they got one point. But in all fairness, you can't really give a wrong answer. The probes fish out the memory and force the brain to recant it in full detail.

Each point earned was irrelevant, but to answer a question right you had to know exactly what they wanted to hear. If you didn't answer with the crucial details that fully expose the sick memory that they had pulled up, then the recovery software goes to work. Every forced sweep causes immeasurable pain and damage to the precious chromosomes needed to play the game. Being honest and being quick were the only real ways to win. They usually started off small, usually stuff about your youth, but if the questions snowballed and the contestant gets caught up in a lie, things could get ugly quick. The key to winning the game was unflinching honesty. Or, so it seemed.

"You have forty-five seconds to answer, Steven, before we electrically centrifuge your memories," Rich said as if he was offering a friend personal tips on saving money with monthly adjusted insurance rates. "What was your most painful sexual experience? Thirty-five seconds."

Don't run the clock. You know what they want to hear...

"I was ten...my sister and I were staying at a cheap hotel with my dad. We went downstate to visit relatives who lived on the coast. The hotel we were staying at had a tiny indoor pool with a small floral green jacuzzi attached. My dad never usually let us go swimming alone, but this time he did. Once we got the okay, my sister and I ran down the long maroon hallways like we were on fire. We splashed and played for hours. My sister, being younger but not *smaller* than me, eventually got tired and left to find food.

"For the first time ever, I was alone in a pool. The coast was clear, so I climbed into the hot tub, a thing my dad usually scolded me for. He always said that the hot tub was for drunk, middle-aged married couples who swing, not for little kids. But, in that moment, I didn't care. I let the icy hotness run over my skin as I fully submerged into the bubbling waters of the jacuzzi. I liked the pressured jets and flashing lights that lined the interior of the oval shaped tub. Never had I felt so free—so independent. I turned to reset the touch dial for a longer play time when—it happened.

"A tingly pressure brushed across the front of my trunks. I knew what was happening, but...I just couldn't stop myself. The option to wait out the stiffness I was feeling never even crossed my mind. Alone and curious, there was only one thing left to do. Slowly, I pulled down my trunks and stuck my beluga whale right into one of the jets. Careful not to get stuck, I tested the snugness of the hole and wiggled my way in. After a few hard pumps, I felt a warm wave rush through my body. I liked the feeling at first—gallons of hot, soapy water shooting up my pisser. My bladder swelled with recycled liquid, but I barely noticed. In that moment, I was livin' free."

Baking like a slab of slated haddock under the hundreds of constellated stage lights, Steven jerked against his straps at the memory. The audience barely noticed him on the other side of the life-size hologram accurately portraying the embarrassing scene—his body twitching and convulsing with each subtle glitch.

"Later, we all went out to dinner. When I eventually got

up to go use the can and take a piss, I nearly passed out from the pain. It felt like someone had shoved a long sewing needle up my dickhole and refused to pull it back out. I constantly had to piss, but when I tried, nothing would come out. And any time something did, it was only hot, stingy dribbles of milky liquid. I cried quietly in the shitter that night, wondering how I was going to explain to my family why I needed to go to the hospital. But, in the end, I couldn't bring myself to do it. I was too embarrassed to ever admit what I did and decided to walk out the pain. For two weeks after that I couldn't take a whiz without tearing up from the excruciating pain—"

Buzzers and random lights blared as the distant crowd was cued to excitedly cheer. Steven tried lazily to turn his head towards all the frantic buzzing, but the wires in his skull limited his motion.

"Well done, Steven," Rich said with not nearly enough fake enthusiasm. "That memory was crucial to unearth for a proper rehabilitation. I'm sure everyone at home can agree that depraved sexual behavior leads to a life of crime. And a life of crime gets you nothing but pain, kids. Alright, Steven. Here is your next question."

Rich fell silent to let the tension build as the floating teleprompter slid into his line of sight.

"Second question… What was your worst recurring nightmare as a child?"

Steven knew the answer—knew it better than anything

else in his life. Slowly, the long, constant string of night terrors from his youth unrolled before him. Dreams so rancid, so soul-shatteringly awful, they often lingered into the waking darkness of his pitch-black room. He remembered spending countless hours hiding from them under cold sheets—the feeling of boney fingers lightly dancing over the thin shielding of blankets wrapped around his shivering body. This lasted from when Steven was eight to twenty-one years old. He was lucky to get more than four hours of real sleep before springing back to life, covered in sweat and clutching for something real. It wasn't until Steven learned to ritually baste those horrible dreams in a steady flow of cheap liquor and hard drugs that he could go a full night without seeing that...*Thing*. Even his last year in prison had been fairly comfy. Not the greatest junk in the world, but certainly good enough for the likes of him. Needless to say, it didn't take him long at all to sniff out the loose powder in that filthy rat box.

Never having told anyone about these nightmares before, Steven now had to force his mind to revive the hazy, dormant dreams of his youth for the hungry studio audience to cannibalize. Trying to wet his lips with the abrasive roughness of his dry tongue, a loose flap of skin dangled annoyingly from the edge of his bottom lip. He knew the questions would be hard, but he wasn't ready for this. It was like someone just handed him a shovel and said, *"There. Dig there,"* while pointing to the haunted graveyard of his past.

Steven didn't want to dig up all those corpses, the ones years of junk and booze helped him bury. But if he didn't dig now, the software would.

Reluctantly, he spoke.

"I'm in my grandfather's house. The sun hangs outside the old turnstile windows facing the countryside. It has a dusty grayish tint, an ashen shine. The light coming off it feels filtered, like the real sun was hiding behind a dirty lamp shade or pane of iced glass. I survey the room I'm currently standing in and suddenly feel like I'm not alone… Someone else is there with me…"

Pausing, Steven felt his shovel hit something hard—heavy. It moved, scraping aside loose dirt. He suddenly realized that the bones were digging their way up towards him. Fast. After all these years of sedation, they wanted badly to be free again.

Physical fingers spasming as his mind's eye watched little white teeth start to sprout their way up through the gaping mouth of dark soil, Steven whimperingly continued.

"I look around the room. A couple of old handmade rocking chairs and an ancient, tubed television are right where they should be, but something isn't right. Suddenly, I am all too aware of my body. A throbbing burn spreads in my chest as I walk over to the grey wooden staircase leading to the second floor. I look to the top of the stairs from where I stand at the base and at first see nothing but an empty door frame. Then, as I mount the first step up, a face slowly appears in the dense square of open darkness. I jolt to a stop and lock eyes with the disembodied scowl looking down at me from the top of the stairs. A long, crudely shaped face glares down at me. Both pitted eyes squirming with juicy worms and maggots.

"Frozen in place, I can only stare back in abstract terror. Its eyes are empty sockets that weep thick purple globs of puss—pooling around the mass of dancing bugs tunneling in and out of its taut skin. In the center of the false face is a pulpy, squashed nose, not dissimilar to the business end of a chewed-up cigar stogie. From where I stand, I can hear its wet leather skin cracking; its open gash of a mouth sucking and gnawing on its own tattered lips."

That was it; Steven could not bring himself to go any further. Right there, in front of everyone, he had officially lost the game.

The holographic projection of the tattered head's guttural, hissing words traveled boundlessly through the grey world of dreams, coming from everywhere and nowhere inside the large studio.

"*KILLIT,*" the thing whispered in stereophonic sound.

Inside Steven's mind and on the lighted stage, static echoes darted away into a borderless space. The image on the platform in front of the audience began to flicker as Steven's mind reflexively suppressed the distressing dream. Too horrified to go on, Steven slumped back against his cage as the recovery software started its job and dutifully supplied the rest.

The face's chewed-up lips continued to flap and tear at every sinister repetition. Demonic chants filled every inch of Steven's receptive brain. A bent, filth-covered appendage, too contorted to be a leg or arm, pounded down with a wet *SLAP!* onto the first lighted step. Another slimy stump soon joined it, followed by another. A mass shape started to take form behind the floating head—large and contorted. Throbbing with confusion, Steven's lidless eyes bulged as the dangling mass slowly descended from the top step.

A scabbed and bloated torso balanced on four razor wire legs sluggishly crawled its way into the light. The vein popped belly skin on the almost human torso was cracked and oozing just like the disfigured face. Armless, its elongated skull bobbed on nubby shoulders with each heavy step. Steven's brain could hardly process any of this, causing the holographic projection to rapidly flicker again.

Just then, he saw it—one of the creature's legs wasn't a leg at all. Being dragged slowly down each uncarpeted step was the corded body of a dying fetus. The fetus' eyes were pit-less black marbles shoved deep into the shallow sockets of its soft, dented skull. Cheesy green skin wilting off in splintered chunks at every new step, its slow descent left a gelatinous trail of greying slime behind.

"*KILLIT!*" the leathery face screeched at Steven from halfway up the stairs. From where he stood, he could see the trailing umbilical cord pulse and slither with unknown nutrients. Through paralyzed lips, Steven's psyche screamed at him to run—to wake up and escape before it was too late. Suddenly, the mucus-covered fetus fell to the fifth step and stopped. Bruised face upturned to his, its features were distinctly different than before.

Its stony face with tiny oil spill eyes was no longer there. Instead, he now saw his own face mirrored back at him.

On the main stage, Steven's body violently spasmed and convulsed against its restraints. Without warning, the projection screens went completely dark—transmission lost. Eyes fluttering wildly, Steven's arms and legs began to shake harder under the steel shackles. The exposed portion of his brain bubbled and sizzled like a greased skillet, causing some steaming cranial liquid to drip down his forehead— stinging his flickering eyes. Smoke and sparks popped off the sharp embedded prongs as the crowd murmured, becoming audibly uneased. Biting clear through his tongue and tearing off a part of his bottom lip, Steven seizured as the pop and sizzle of his brain grew louder. In seconds, a glistening goatee of blood slowly spread over his gnarled lips and chin—his fused skull now a live cherry bomb.

A short siren went off, and soon Steven's body was still once again. His holographic heart monitor projected a deadline. As crew members shambled onto the stage to unload and remove his crispy corpse, Rich subtly cued for the softer lights and coolly turned to address the audience.

"Well, folks, there you have it. Another tortured soul

released of his mortal sins and guilt," Rich empathetically cooed as the crowd hushed to receive his teleprompted opinion. His flashy game show host persona was momentarily ditched for a more somber, elegant tone. "According to Steven's records, his mother died tragically while birthing him. Clearly, this guilt never left Steven, maybe even pushed him straight into a life of crime. So sad…so very sad…." His padded shoulders shrugged in a sympathetic gesture that said, *Oh well, tough break, kid. Better luck next time.*

"According to Steven's personal file, he had these horrid nightmares for most of his life. So, let this man's demise be a grave lesson to us all. Had he been taking the regulated dosage of government supplied Ubikorin— America's #1 anti-depressant and mood regulator—then this whole tragedy could have been avoided. His mind shouldn't have fought the recovery software. All the pain we just saw was most surely self-inflicted. The refusal to confront his guilt about his mother caused the violent death we all just witnessed here tonight. Sometimes even the best therapy fails the ones who need it most. But you know what they say, a man can only change in his heart if the spirit is also willing. A true example of how powerful the mind can be if not properly medicated.

"Steven came here looking for freedom from the sins he committed, and gosh darnit, that's exactly what we gave him. Ain't that right, folks?!"

Rowdy applause filled every inch of the packed studio. Loud rhythmic music suddenly joined the surge, and the atmosphere of death was effortlessly replaced with one of joyful celebration.

"Until next time, this is Rich Richardson saying: From Rags to Redemption; where there's a will, *there's a way*! Sleep tight, and good night."

As the screen slowly faded to black, a small line of glowing white print lined the bottom curve of the blank screen:

Sponsored by Ubikorin LTD and partners. All rights reserved.

A KISS IS A KISS

Actually, I do remember my first kiss. It happened way back when I was in fourth grade.

I was sitting alone at the swing set during afternoon recess, hairless potbelly stretched full with the digestive bubbling of a recent hot lunch. Nothing special, just the cafeteria-served beans 'n franks that I willfully ate every other day. Due to my sensitive stomach, it was about the only thing on the school menu that I could keep down.

I vividly remember that it was a cold April afternoon. The dark coverage of ashy clouds misted cold showers so thin that the falling particles of rain seemed to just sit on air—motionless holograms of frozen light. It gave the passing breeze an odd density that filled my lungs with heavy beads of dew—little glass crystals and slivers that stung with each shallow breath. Other children in colorful windbreakers ran back and forth through the gated lot like cattle on speed. Every quick movement made a loud *swish-swish* sound that sliced through the steady drone of surrounding laughter. Not me, though. I just sat aside and watched—barely making an effort to push myself on the solitary swing. Kids would randomly dart by every couple of seconds or so, but no one ever stopped or noticed me. I was just another part of the playground: a piece of inanimate equipment to avoid running into.

No one noticed me, except for the small group of girls curiously staring from across the yard.

In unison, they all mercilessly chanted, "David Doughie! David Doughie!"

Five in all, they stood in a loose circle by the edge of the red brick wall. Sporting matching pigtails with color coordinated scrunchies, they were of one thought—one mind. Like a small hive of honeybees without a queen, their constant buzzing and feeding proved that they weren't incapable of much more than rudimentary thought. Only able to do the most intermediate of tasks, each action was an involuntary reflex—a brain spasm. Sure, they could eat solid foods, walk upright, and regurgitate random factoids on command as any functioning human could do, but it was all a mirroring gesture. Destined to forever play a lifelong game of monkey see, monkey do. Yet, at that time, I felt they were infinitely more capable than I.

More real—more human.

When the insectual hive noticed my returning glance from the lonely skeleton of the swing set, the laughing and mocking began. This was a ritualistic hazing I had come to expect every recess. They would hurl insults and funny faces from their side of the playground like mortar rounds, each shot intended to not only maim, but kill. Other kids occasionally joined in on the jokes too, but most times it was just the same group of dead eyed girls with the bratty ponytails and cruel smiles. I sorta understood why they chose to target me out of all the others; I was an easy target and never posed any serious threat of retaliation. When the fangs came out, my first reaction was to flop on my back and go belly up. Like a true coward, the very idea of conflict made me physically ill to the point where I'd rather get my guts ripped out than face my tormentors.

Staying true to the old saying, "God hates a coward."

Why do I let them do this? I'd ask myself, mentally turtling away when the high-pitched laughter became too shrill to endure any longer. *No wonder they hate me. They know I'm not like them. They know I don't belong here…*

Clearly, my self-ostracization made no sense to any of them. Being willfully withdrawn and shy is so counterproductive when you consider how socially driven we are as a species. In fact, I would even go as far as to argue that all species, not just humans, are fundamentally tethered by social interactions within their kind. But if this stands to be inherently true of all creatures…then why didn't I feel that same instinctual connection? Was I simply born without the other end of that common thread? Whatever the reason might be, I felt that my inherent faults were painfully obvious—a spiritual defect that deserved to be ridiculed and shamed by all.

So, before I even had a chance to really live, I was already confiding in the fact that I would someday die. Alone.

And to only add another layer to the grand irony that was my childhood at the time, I knew I was miserable because I had no friends—yet I didn't try to play or interact with any of the other kids. Couldn't. I probably came across as being stuck-up or snotty to them as a result. That counts as irony, right?

Looking away from the cruel huddle of venomous jeers, I watched a lone girl slowly make her way across the woodchip filled lot. Entranced by her subtle movements—much more graceful and poised than all the others—I gazed intently as her stride was broken and became intercepted by the group. Caught in the crossfire, their mean-spirited heckling was soon turned on her. In a false crescendo, they chanted, *"Kiss the ginger! Kiss the ginger!"* While viewing the live spitfire, I suddenly realized that I recognized the lone girl from art class. Like me, she was another quiet kid—never one for boisterous behavior, unlike most of our peers. Her name might have been Melissa, but I can't be sure now. Sadly, we had never gotten the chance to formerly talk to one another. Melissa and her family moved away the next year to the West Coast—Seattle, I think? Or maybe it was Portland.

Anyway, Melissa and I both silently suffered through

each long school day until the merciful clanging of the bell dismissed us back into the wild where we belonged. I can't recall ever hearing her speak aloud the whole time we were in school together, but then again, I wasn't much of a talker either. Whenever we'd get assigned to group painting projects or study groups, I'd always position myself in just the right chair so I could sneak longing glances at her from across the table. Drinking in every subtle line and curve of her beautifully sculpted face, I couldn't help but wonder if she kept her true self inside for the same reasons that I did.

I wondered, *Was she missing that one string, too?*

It was because of this notion that I felt compelled to stand up from that swing and defend her. Melissa was like me—an outcast. Reserved and misunderstood. Whether she realized it or not, we had an unspoken kinship—a bond. And it was this internal connection that urged me to stand up, march across the schoolyard, and strike those other girls down.

If not for Melissa, then for our kind.

But those heroic visions of chivalry lasted all of two seconds before another wave of emotion washed over me. Suddenly, everything inside me tensed up. Like a rubber band stretched beyond its point of elasticity, the tension broke and dispersed—resulting in a deep chested sneeze. Like an overturned volcano, a hot, slimy bomb of snot exploded from the open chasms of my nose. Runny chunks of yellowish goop streamed down my chin, lining my lips in a thin coating of vile stickiness. Reflexively, I tried my best to wipe the mess off on my jacket sleeve, but the sheer material of my windbreaker did little but further spread it around. And even though I kept wiping and wiping at it, a glistening mask of shining mucus and phlegm remained.

This didn't go unnoticed by the huddled mass of nasty little women across the way. They continued to point and laugh at me—their attention divided but cruel wit still laser sharp.

Ew! Gross!

That's so sick!

What a spazz!

This went on for several more moments until—it happened. The lone girl, clearly fed up with all the teasing, finally caved. Briskly, she broke off from the encompassing group and headed across the playground in my direction.

But by the time I looked up from the swing and meekly peered into Melissa's pink face, it was too late. Before I had time to react to her nearing presence, she lunged at me. Like two hairy fists wrapped in wet deli meat, our faces slapped together with a hard *clap!* that could be heard from all four corners of the playground. The sickening *clink* of my teeth hitting hers—a sharp, unfeeling sound that reminded me of two ball bearings striking each other in a game of marbles— made me physically wince in pain. A dull *thud* punched at the thick plate in the back of my head upon full impact, sending a shower of white stars cascading behind my eyes.

Muscles so tense that they felt like they might snap my bones to ivory splinters under my skin, the unexpected collision left me paralyzed with unparalleled uncertainty. In that moment, I couldn't process any of what was happening. It all felt so strange—everything from the physical contact to the odd new sensation rolling through my shivering body.

Her relative mass pushing into my own made me feel less solid—porous, like a giant sponge or lump of uncooked dough. I remember thinking that if she pushed herself hard enough, we'd forcibly meld together. Fusing into one body. Half of the mutant mass would be her and the other me. In my mind, I could literally see and feel our organs and limbs tangling and breaking against each other in the shift. I imagined the sound would be something like two live pigs being tossed into a giant air compressor until they both popped into meat confetti.

To this day, the lingering thought still makes me cringe a little.

In the blink of an eye, those sickening impulses came and went. All that was left was the sour taste of distrust, incomprehension, and drying snot on my cracked lips. Even at the tender age of ten, I knew that this kiss didn't mean anything. This wasn't about any hidden adorations or schoolyard crushes; Melissa was only doing what was needed to get those girls to stop teasing me. Or, more likely, to get them to stop teasing her. I couldn't decide which, with the alien touch and swelling pain rushing across my sticky lips, but I knew it wasn't love.

Never was—never would be.

In seconds, the kiss was over. Not once did I feel that spark of fiery passion that everyone's supposed to experience with their first. No, all I felt were two hard lips mashed to my own—void of all subtextual meaning. After Melissa pulled away from me, fully breaking our slimy bond, she took a step back and spat loudly on the ground at my feet. Without saying a word, she turned and walked stonily back across the playground.

And as I watched her walk away—glistening mouth left slightly agape in shock—I suddenly choked and threw up my lunch all over the front of my windbreaker. Tongue petrified to a piece of old shoe leather, a nervous tick completely dried out my mouth and throat. Now rocking steadily on the swing, I coughed and retched uncontrollably; fat cheeks flaring while my mouth and nose spewed more stringy bodily fluids. Through watery eyes, I watched as the last few spoonfuls of my lunch soaked into the woodchips below—leaving only a wet spot of gelatinous brown and pink sludge.

Gargling like a mamma seal protecting its young, I sat swinging and gagging until the playground monitor forced me to go inside and visit the nurse. And like that, it was all over, the memory forever stored in my head to be replayed over and over again until there is no one left to revive it.

But hey, a kiss is a kiss…

THE PRINCIPALITY

[The following text is an audio transcript of a segment from the cult-classic late night paranormal talk radio show *Shadow Dance Radio*. While the original recording can be found through grainy bootlegs, much of the audio is indecipherable and of very poor quality. The following transcript is reported to be the infamous call in its entirety as it was aired on the morning of June 11, 1993.]

LARRY:

Welcome back, listeners! As always, this is your host Larry Moore, your guide through the terrifying, yet irresistibly entertaining, black abyss known only as *Shadow Dance Radio*. At the start of the hour, I opened up the lines to let some of you call in and share your thoughts and experiences with all things supernatural, and while the last caller's story about her clairvoyant cat who could predict winning Powerball numbers was very interesting, right now I'd like to switch gears and see if we can get someone to call in with a story or experience that's truly spooky.

Come on, people, I want to hear something so bone chilling that I won't need this second cup of coffee to get me through the rest of the hour.

[Break for loud sipping sound]

Ah, I see by the blinking phonelines that I've already enticed a few of you. Let's go to the lines and see what we got.

Hello, this is Larry Moore of *Shadow Dance Radio*, you're on the air, caller.

CALLER:

[loud feedback noise]
Hello? Hello? Is anyone there?

LARRY:

Yes, but caller, please do us all a kindness and turn off your radio. I'll stay on the line, don't worry.

CALLER:

[loud thump followed by faint clicking sounds]

159

Oh, sorry. This better?

LARRY:

Yes. Now, what's your name and where are you calling from, sir?

CALLER:

My name isn't important and I'd rather not say where I'm presently located. My time is precious, so if it's okay with you I'd like to—

LARRY:

That's fine, caller. I get where you're coming from. I wouldn't want the missus catching me out this late, either.

[soft laughter]

So, what paranormal or supernatural story do you have to share with my audience tonight? A story of ghosts, goblins, or astral projection? Maybe a random Bigfoot encounter—

CALLER:

Shut up, you braindead imbecile! I have

to share with you and your listeners the awful prophecy of self-implosion that will unfold within the next twenty-five years! I've tried contacting various media outlets and even the military to warn everyone, but no one would listen to me after the words "time traveler" left my mouth. Your program is my last hope to get some sort of word out about what is to come if we as a people don't change our ways.

LARRY:

Well, okay then. I don't appreciate the salty language, but you certainly got my attention. Time traveler, huh? Now, that's very interesting stuff right there. What year did you travel here from, caller? Assuming you aren't from a different dimensional plane entirely.

CALLER:

Originally, I came from the year 1963, or at least that's when I first traveled from. God, that feels like a century ago now. Anyway, I was chief engineer of the D39GO operation in…

LARRY:

The what and what? Sounds like the name of a side character in one of those *Star Wars* movies. I heard just last week that Lucas was on board to make three more of those. Did you happen to catch a sneak peek at any of those on your visit to the future, caller? I'm sure my listeners would love to hear all about—

CALLER:

Quiet! Have you no sense of urgency?! Where was I? Oh, right...I was directly involved in a top-secret military project that dealt mainly in advanced theoretical physics and weaponry. The unit I oversaw was so secret that even J. Edgar himself didn't know of its existence. Although no one would come out and say this outright, the project was primarily established to reverse engineer remnants of what was believed to be a primitive tachyon flux spectrometer that was supposedly designed by the Nazis and seized by the U.S. military after the conclusion of World War II. The Krauts destroyed most of the components to the machine before we could snatch it up, but lucky for us, German orderliness came out in our favor. While in a frenzy to destroy the machine, they forgot to burn the blueprints. So, with only the blueprints and endless government funding, it took nearly twenty years and thirty scientists to complete enough of the contraption to begin testing. Being almost entirely sure the damn thing wouldn't work on its first try, I foolishly volunteered to sit in the driver's seat—

LARRY:

Whoa, driver's seat? Was this time machine a car or something? Like in the movie *Back to the Future*? Man, I love that movie! Do you remember the part where Doc looks over at Marty and says...

CALLER:

No! Stop interrupting me, you hair-brained jackass!

It wasn't a car, but we did use a bucket seat from a broken-down Ford pickup we found at the local scrapyard as the main seating for the unit. The machine was of a single person design, much like a fighter jet cockpit, with shielded sides and a main control console directly in front. We named it H.G. after H.G. Wells. It was eerie how similar this thing came out looking like the apparatus described in *The Time Machine*. If I didn't know any better, I would swear the Germans designed it with Wells in mind.

Anyway, I foolishly volunteered for the first test run. Had I known the damn thing would actually work, I would've made Herzog or Gates do it, but I was so certain that it wouldn't even power up. I gotta give it to the Germans, though, for their impeccable note-keeping. In my thirty years as chief engineer of the Meta-Science Unit in the United States military, I have never seen a mechanism of such flawless complexity. Every single part, right down to the framing, was impeccably designed. The joke when we first started the project was that Hitler used the machine to escape capture just before its destruction. With a mud-stained swastika on his sleeve, he was probably back in the Stone Age teaching cavemen to Sieg Heil and goosestep.

When the machine initially started up, I was so stunned that I just sat there and watched the knobs twirl and the landscape melt all around me. All too late did I realize that my ignorant cynicism for the impossible would send me hurdling to the future.

LARRY:

And that date happened to be 1993? Oh come on, thirty years into the future isn't that long of a stretch. I don't know about you, caller, but if I was part of a top-secret military operation, I would probably be on file somewhere as working for the government before my untimely disappearance. The military must have been able to put two and two together and figure out that you took off with the machine to the future. Why can't you just go to them and say, "Hey, it's me and I am stuck in the future," or something?

CALLER:

> I already said that I tried to contact the government, but due to the ultra-classified nature of what I was involved in, my identification files and disappearance must've been covered up and forgotten. I basically signed my life away when I came onto the project and swore an oath of secrecy.

> Also, I didn't punch in 1993, I accidentally put 2016. Which is why I am on your show tonight—

LARRY:

> 2016?! Cheese and crackers! Well, folks, I asked for your best and that's what I got. I have many questions, but I know you're limited on time—

CALLER:

> Like I was saying, once the machine powered down and I could stop vomiting long enough to take in my new surroundings, I quickly deduced that I was in some sort of landfill or dump. After about ten minutes of rolling around like a

sick dog, I gathered myself up and got back into the machine and set the dials for 1963. When nothing happened, my heart dropped. I jumped out of the cockpit and ran to the back to inspect the battery containment unit. There, pooling at the ground around my feet in a fluorescent sludge, was the coolant for the battery casing. Whether it overheated and cracked somehow in travel or simply aged with the passing years was unknown to me, but I knew I wasn't going anywhere until I found a way to patch it up.

Thinking fast, I quickly stacked a pile of soiled mattresses around H.G. to keep anyone from accidentally coming across it or further damaging it by mistake. With around one hundred dollars in small bills at my disposal, I set out of the dump to gather supplies.

On my seven mile walk to the nearest town, I wondered tirelessly about why H.G. didn't land at its original location on the air base, seeing as how the machine doesn't physically move on solid ground but dissimilates and slides through the fabric of time. Upon further thought, I eventually chalked up the miscalculation to the Earth's constant rotation and shifting tectonic plates, undoubtedly sliding past me whilst I was suspended in a semi-solid state for so many decades.

I was initially worried that I had slid too far, possibly onto foreign soil where my paper money would be no good. To my rough calculations, I was around 10.7 miles from the base. That is, if it was even still there anymore.

Once I got to town I visited the first retail store that I could find and browsed their tools with great success. Among the many bonds and adhesives that were available, I also found patches and coolant that would do the job just fine. While the prices on these things were ridiculous, I calculated that I had just enough money to buy all I needed to repair the damaged unit and get home. With such a sudden turnaround in luck, I decided to be a little adventurous and browsed the rest of the massive store to see what else the future held.

The first thing I noticed was that people didn't look much different from my time. I assumed the fashions would be more *futuristic* and sleeker, but the differences were much more subtle than I had anticipated. The only notable thing I gathered from the clambering crowd around me was how in sync with each other they were. Like a school of fish caught in a strong undercurrent, the vast number of them streamed to and fro—always clustered in groups. While some seemed to have a purpose in their stride, others simply stood slouched over some random colorfully packaged do-dad, drooling and yammering to the others in their group. Even with the huge aisleways to walk through, I was constantly bumping into random parties of people who seemed to be just loitering about with no discernable goal. Loudly shouting hyphenated gibberish, they smacked their greasy lips at each other while ignoring the flabby bodies all around them.

I was frantically apologizing and moving over for passersby, noticing that not one person so much as faintly acknowledged my presence. At one point, I accidentally knocked over a middle aged woman with a full cart of groceries, but when I quickly apologized and began helping her up from the floor, she scrambled to her feet and ran away screaming, leaving a pile of oversized produce and other shiny objects in the middle of the crowded aisle to be stomped on. In seconds, the food and gadgets were flattened into a colorless mush by the passing stampede of feet.

From there, I eventually shoved my way over to the electronics department. Immediately, I noticed the huge wall of beautifully colored screens at the very back of the long aisle, each one showing a stunningly clear image of something impossible. The random pictures hypnotically filtered in and around the screen in a dazzling show of light. The urge to gaze at those anamorphic lights was so strong at one point that I had to step back against the crowd and close my eyes.

After my brief sensory overload faded into an anxious quiver in my chest, I walked over to the great wall. Forcing myself to concentrate on just one of the hundreds of screens, I leaned in close and squinted my eyes against the surrounding glare.

On it was a shot of a man and woman sitting at a news desk. All around them were electric words and thumbnail images—tiny screens inside of screens. Flashing and blinking in and out of frame while the two people sat and talked at the camera. I couldn't hear what they were saying, so I found the volume switch on the side of the thin black frame and turned it up enough to hear over the crowd.

What I heard was worse than any nightmare imaginable.

Flying robots controlled by the government are used for spying on ordinary people.

Terrorist groups from various world regions are all simultaneously trying to destroy America.

Cops love shooting black people.

Suicide rates among teens have risen thirty percent since last year.

A woman with blue hair talking about a woman's right to have an imaginary penis.

A socialist, a woman, and a real estate agent are all running for the presidency at the same time.

A woman with a penis talking about a woman's right to not be forced to use a certain bathroom in public.

Advertisement disguised as news followed by supposedly random comments about said advertisement.

Cutest ugly dog contest.

Various unofficial opinions on what may or may not be breaking news.

Millions of homeless people can't afford food but have access to portable phones and free needles.

Unconfirmed celebrity gossip followed by a story about a mass shooting.

Man with orange skin and wheat colored cotton candy hair answering questions about a giant theoretical wall across the Mexican border.

Candy laced with marijuana is sold out of vending machines.

Sexy advertisement for Breast Cancer Research.

Children brutally killing their own parents then taking pictures with the corpses to later share with their friends.

A famous Olympian athlete that no one cared about for decades intentionally mutilates his penis and is now deemed a hero by all.

Activist groups protest the First Amendment by using said Amendment to protest.

A woman with a low-cut shirt and exposed cleavage talks about something called *Rape Culture.*

Government bails out major banks after declaring 3.7 trillion-dollar debt to China.

Etc. Etc.

For the next four hours, I stood perfectly still—body practically petrified to stone—and watched this one screen, trying my hardest to absorb and configure the seemingly endless flow of *vital information*, until eventually a blunt-faced employee forced me to buy my things and leave. On my long walk back to the dump, I had a lot of time to think about the horrific things I had seen and heard, all the time questioning if any of this was even real, when it hit me.

I had seen all of this before.

Shortly after the end of WWII, a close colleague of mine recommended the book *1984* by George Orwell, saying that it was one of the most unsettling novels he had ever read. Intrigued by his claim, I acquired a copy and, while I enjoyed the bleak writing style, I thought the story as a whole was a vast exaggeration of man's own capacity for self-enslavement. While I got the symbolism of Big Brother and Newspeak, I simply chose not to consider this scenario ever playing out in any future country on Earth where man has already had a taste of freedom.

LARRY:

Hate to tell you this, caller...but I've actually never read *1984*. Oh, I did see some of the movie on cable once. Seriously, though, I don't know what to make of any of this. Are you trying to say that in a future America people are willingly enslaved by their own government? No offense, caller, but there are people who say this has been going on since the beginning of the Cold War. How is this future timeline any different from now?

CALLER:

Don't you get it?! Somehow, we as a human race have become so overly stimulated and reliant on mass media enterprises to think for us that individual conquest has become nothing more than a glutinous blob of semi-coherent self-worship and narcissistic boasting. While I'll admit, intellectualism has never really been a staple of American society since the time of our founding fathers, the atrocities I've witnessed were nothing less than a global pandering to the most primitive impulses of what make us human. For every actual news story I witnessed, there were thousands—perhaps millions—of subtle and not so subtle subliminal messages streaming seamlessly under the thin layer of illuminated false importance: a non-stop barrage of thoughts and words being slammed into my skull with each passing second.

I could see that just like in Orwell's dystopian hellscape people were brought up to think that individual thought and character are something to be feared, not celebrated. If you're different, then you're unknown to others around you. In the end, that kind of conscious deviance only adds up to one thing—bigotry. Concentrating too much on our superficial differences and not on what is truly important, individualism is seen as more of a mental illness than a personality trait. Anyone with a varying opinion to yours must be considered a threat and therefore must not be tolerated, right? Being your own man means stepping away from the mass majority. But if you choose to do so then you must be a villain; why else would you decide to break from the safety of the herd in the first place? What better way to control an entire race of people than convincing them that the world is fundamentally perfect and about to explode all at the same time. With constant fear of annihilation mixed with an overinflated sense of everlasting self-importance, the people of 2016 are doomed to self-implode.

Only after I left the store did I realize the reason for the mass groupings of ill-mannered boobs wasn't an isolated incident. It was a common mindset. These people were conditioned to never be alone, as to avoid any real self-reflection or questioning of differing ethics. When faced with the vast knowledge of the entire world so readily available to anyone who wishes to view it, one person can only remain humble for so long before eventually caving to the overwhelming fact that the world is now flat. The mysteries and allure of traveling abroad and experiencing cultures outside of your own have been stomped by the mighty boot of fear mongering and over simplification that seems to be flowing out of those screens at an ever-expanding rate.

We as a species cannot spend every waking moment being comforted by our vices and familiarity to what we consider to be everyday occurrences, but in actuality are fabricated lies tailormade to keep us docile. What we have here is a man-made virtual reality where most people voluntarily sacrifice their willpower and identity for convenience and technology. Living a life through a mass connection of invisible wires, punching imaginary words and pictures into a not so tangible space where their vanity will hopefully live on for all eternity. The things they do and say will undoubtedly outlive the entire human race by eons. Infinite recognition and validation of anyone's existence will be as easy as tying your shoes or pouring a glass of milk. With all these means of self-expression and ignorant opinions being held to such high reverence, one can't help but set themselves up on a soapbox and inflate their egos to the point of combustion.

Can you even imagine a world where trivial things like cordless phones and celebrity opinions take precedence over senseless death and human suffering? Can you fathom a world where you have to question everything you experience because faucets of false reality are manufactured daily? I say true philosophy died the way of the dodo bird. Slow and unnoticed.

LARRY:

Okay...then why travel back to 1993? Why not just go back to 1963 and get an even earlier head start on warning the public?

CALLER:

Damnit, I didn't have a choice! After I snuck back into the dump and fixed the coolant case, worse news came. The fueling agent that powers H.G. was too low for me to make it all the way back to my original time. 1993 is as far back as I could go. I'm terrified to think that I might live to see this world turn sour. Again.

The people need to know before it's too late; we still have time to correct ourselves. If we just live in moderation and stop this strange virtue signaling, we may be able to curb this before—

LARRY:

Well, folks, you heard it here first! In the year 2016, we will all be mindless sheep with portable phones. Hopefully they are better than the bricks we have nowadays, am I right, folks? Hey, caller, did you happen to get a look at one of these fancy future phones?

CALLER:

Have you heard a single word I've said?! If we don't stop this way of being, the entire species will inevitably fail! The entire United States—no, the *WORLD*— is at risk of regressing back to the days of totalitarian ruling! We all need to question what is going—

[INTRO MUSIC SLOWLY FADES IN]

LARRY:

Well, you know what that music means, ladies and gents. It's time to go to another commercial break. Thanks for the story, caller, and good luck with saving the future.

[soft laughter]

181

We will be back to take more of your calls after these messages. Stayed tuned, friends.

[While this call is held by some to be proof of time travel and the intentional deterioration of our moral fiber, skeptics claim that it is merely just a lucky shot in the dark by a deranged man with a prophecy loosely based on an outdated science fiction novel. Numerous memes and re-tweets of this conversation have caused it to trend in the last couple of months, leaving many of us to ask the question #Isit2late?]

GRAMPY

Quentin took a sip from the sweating glass of cheap whiskey as he watched lines and colors dance across the dusty surface of his ancient TV screen, pebbles of ice tapping against his dentures as he drank. The honey-colored liquid no longer burned his throat after so many years of the same afternoon routine. The Sox were well in the lead against the Yankees, top of the sixth, which was the kind of action that used to excite Quentin. But, sadly, an eerie sense of familiarity had etherized the whole experience.

For a moment, he pried his greying eyes away from the screen and glanced at the empty sun-faded recliner to his left. Really, he should've gotten rid of it after Geneva died six years prior.

Gone an' turned tah dust, Quentin thought bitterly as he slammed more of the whiskey down his gullet. He wasn't thirsty, but his old, decrepit body demanded relief from those painful thoughts of times that were. In his own selfish way, Quentin hated his late wife for dying of lung cancer after almost fifty years of blissful marriage together. Not for leaving him alone, but for taking his heart to the ground with her.

He had his chair and she had hers. It was always hers, no one else's. Even after Geneva left in the most unpleasant of ways, none of the extended family that came to visit Quentin over the years would sit in that chair. Yet, here it remained. And still each day, as he had done since the day she died, Quentin yanked the dingy tapestry off the chair's back, cursing under his breath about the hideousness of the damn thing as he chucked it into a far corner. Knitted by Geneva's mother back in the cruel New England winter of 1939, Quentin couldn't remember a single day of his adult life that he didn't have to stare at that god-awful piece of euro-trash every time he entered the room.

Probably made of ol' Gypsy hair n' wild ergot or some shit, Quentin often thought sourly. He never told Geneva how he really felt about the family heirloom, only prayed that one of their eight kids would rip or stain or burn the damn thing so he could finally throw it out. Fifty long years later, no dice. The kids all grew up and left, gaining much needed distance between them and that eyesore of a chair.

"Ever'thin' leaves," Quentin mumbled to the puffy yellow squares of stitchings, "… 'cept you…"

At that moment, a new question suddenly arose.

Then why keep pickin' the damn thing up and puttin' it back?!

As the strange thought crept to the forefront of his mind, the pretty Latina sports anchor who did the score updates slid onto the screen. Smiling, her bubblegum lips and curvaceous figure yanked his wandering eyes firmly back into place. Reflexively, Quentin quickly shrugged off the neon magnetism and stood up to bring his now empty glass to the sink.

As was routine.

Rinsing out his cup, his thoughts again wandered to Geneva's chair. *Ya know, I should just throw that damn thing out already. What's the sense in keepin' it? Gahd damnit, 'Neva ain't here no more!*

Soon, warm whiskey again filled his cup. He couldn't remember getting the bottle out from the cupboard under the sink. However, this spatial lapse didn't stop the steady flow of amber liquid. Flat, off-brand diet coke and a single ice cube found their way into his glass next. Quentin forced himself to accept this momentary lapse, but only out of sheer annoyance. Silently—pulled out of time—he shuffled back into the living room and continued to sit.

Every so often, he looked over his shoulder at that yellow blanket and wondered just how it got back up on the chair. But before the answer could come, his eyes met the null glow of the TV.

Slowly, Quentin took a sip from his glass and sighed, *"My brain's gone an' turned tah dust...jus' like evrythin' else...*

A DINNER OF ONIONS

"This is it," Doug murmured to himself, his voice gently reverberating off the corners of the now vacant living room. "Time to bite the big one."

Slowly, he turned in his chair and picked up the .38 snub nose revolver from the coffee table to his left.

The weight of it felt good in his hands, and for a time he simply sat in silence admiring the sandalwood handle and overall fine craftsmanship. The gun had been his father's and, through much legal turmoil, was willed to Doug after his passing five years prior. Doug had never used the gun before. Up until this morning he had never even removed it from the beat-up shoebox that it was not so carefully stashed in. But, given the current state of things, he felt that the time had come.

Doug was ready to die.

Due to numerous bad investments in the late nineties—sinking thousands of dollars into collectable Beanie Babies and stocks for a South Korean company that manufactured novelty cell phones for the elderly—by late 2005 Doug was almost a million dollars in debt. His wife, Maggie, and his two sons, Duke and Gary, stuck by him through the bulk of these unfortunate times. But the loss of his managerial job at the Blockbuster downtown was the nail that tore his sack.

After fifteen years of marriage, Doug woke up that morning to find a tear-stained note crudely taped to the bathroom mirror. The note simply stated that Maggie had filed for divorce behind Doug's back and that she would be taking Duke and Gary to live at her mother's house in Seattle until all the legal documents were finalized. Nowhere in the note did it say why she left or when Doug would get to see his kids again.

Doug didn't need an explanation. He knew why she had left and, furthermore, completely understood. To not acknowledge the massive failure that was his professional life would be an outright lie tailored to no one but himself. A good wife deserves a husband who provides and protects his family from the unforgiving land of no return known as Bankruptcy. It wasn't fair to Maggie or their two sons—both now in their early teens—who would grow up to never know what it was like to not live from day to day, paycheck to paycheck. A father should be the model for his children and, in a sense, an archetype for how they choose to live their lives.

Doug was neither an archetype nor a good father. He was nothing but a broken shell of a man with an empty house full of the things that he temporarily owned until the bank repossessed it all. The meager belongings that Maggie and the boys took that morning were only a fraction of all the mental landmines that he could not avoid while living there. Everywhere he looked, Doug was reminded of the only people he thought would stick by his side no matter how badly he messed up. Only now, in this much needed moment of self-reflection, did he truly see how much of a fool he was and always had been. His life had been nothing but a series of poorly executed business decisions fueled by greed and ignorance. Without his family, he was utterly alone and without direction. His soul ached like an impacted molar—rotten on the inside. The will to get up every day with a big smile and put one foot in front of the other until he reached his grave was completely gone. Nothing was left for him here.

Doug was not a religious man, nor inherently strong-willed, so suicide seemed the most efficient solution to his existential pointlessness. Without attempting to contact Maggie at her mother's, Doug independently decided what needed to be done.

In a way, he had known things would get to this point. He even saw the acquiring of the gun as a sign to throw in the towel. The best Doug could hope for now was that the bullets he found rattling around in the bottom of that dusty old shoebox were still good. He could not afford to buy new ones.

Having read his wife's note, Doug proceeded to get

dressed. He ate a couple pieces of buttered toast for breakfast to settle the gnawing pain in his stomach, but not a morsel more. After toast, he took the gun down from the top shelf of his bedroom closet. Once he had loaded the three bullets he found, he went into the living room and sat in his favorite chair for the last time.

Now, with the gun placed firmly under his chin, he held his breath and slowly applied pressure to the curved trigger.

But just before he could shoot, several loud knocks erupted at the front door.

Caught completely off guard, Doug flinched in his seat—causing the .38 to go off with a deafening boom next to his right ear. A siren of white, hot noise exploded in his brain—momentarily blotting out the world. For a second, Doug was convinced that he accidentally blew off a portion of his own face. Fortunately, the shot missed his head by an inch and instead hit a framed Sears portrait of him and his family dressed in their Sunday bests. With a big smoking hole where his wife's smiling face should have been, Doug took a moment to admire the irony of this image before shakily putting the gun back on the table. Dazed, he quickly stood up and rubbed at his right ear until the incessant ringing was nothing but a distant tone. Through all of this, he couldn't help but wonder who was knocking at his front door with such malice.

With my luck it's probably Maggie with the kids, Doug thought miserably to himself. *Only I could unintentionally time a suicide to further inconvenience everyone's life: the big capper to the epic saga of selfish douche-baggery that is my sorry existence. How am I going to explain a bullet hole in the family portrait? No matter, I doubt she will even notice or care. Maggie would probably welcome the idea if she knew what I was doing. I'm sure she's just here to get more of her shit and probably the kids' old clothes, then it's back to Seattle to enjoy the rest of her life without me around to fuck things up...*

Pacing about the living room trying to figure out what to do, Doug eventually gathered up the pistol, put it in the back waistband of his sweatpants, and composed himself before slowly opening the front door.

Standing there—basking in the warm, orange light of the morning sun—was not Maggie or his sons, but an oddly shaped man in a very outdated pin-stripe suit. A fine powder of grey dust wafted off of his shoulders and sleeves before dissipating into the morning breeze. From the ground up, Doug slowly took in the man's strange appearance. Upon first glance, the stranger reminded him vaguely of a dried-up bullfrog stuffed into an old, hand-me-down three piece suit. An aristocratic amphibian doing its best door-to-door salesman impersonation. With long tendril arms and thin stick-in-the-mud legs, the man was without a doubt the strangest person Doug had ever seen in his life. Crusty yellow eyelids framed his beady, misshapen eyes that seemed to stare in all directions at once. Yet, Doug couldn't help but feel the nagging twinge of dejá vu as he peered through the open door and waited for the inevitable sales pitch or court summons from his new visitor.

In an almost upright squatting position, the man held a briefcase in one scrawny hand while the other adjusted his wide brimmed fedora hat against the beaming sunlight. With his bulbous eyes twitching and lips flapping together, the man stared right through Doug as if entranced by something off in the back of the house. The sound of the man's spastic convulsions—grey teeth clicking and joints popping—were barely audible over the normal noises of birds and distant traffic. Idly, he squirmed and jiggled in this awkward dance for some time until, finally, Doug broke the awkward silence.

One shaky hand still resting on the doorknob, Doug hesitantly asked, "Can…I help you?"

As if prompted, the man stopped jittering and slowly straightened up, resuming his former role as salesman.

"Hello, Doug. I have something very urgent to discuss with you. If it's alright, we could just step inside here—"

Before Doug could react, the man slid one long, shifty leg inside the partially open door and proceeded to jigger passed Doug—pointed feet tapping and spindly legs pumping. Confused and frightened by the sudden intrusion, Doug stepped back and inadvertently allowed the man to bounce into the living room. Once inside, the man spun back around and slapped the front door shut with one life-sized Stretch Armstrong hand, executed a perfect pinwheel somersault into a backflip over Doug's chair and landed gracefully on the couch. Without emotion, the man casually laid his briefcase on the coffee table in front of him.

Still standing motionless by the front door, completely in awe, Doug watched the man in blurry disbelief.

Noticing Doug's stunned demeanor, the man shrilly asked, "What's wrong, Doug? Don't you remember me?" He tilted his head back, cackling in unhinged laughter at Doug's blank stare. His laughter—like a rabid guinea pig placed in front of the world's loudest bullhorn—consisted of short outbursts of high-pitched shrieks. Shrieking so loud that the previous ringing in Doug's ears came back with a vengeance.

When the squawking finally stopped, the man smiled and smoothly said, "Okay...I'm here, you're here, let's do this." He then leaned over and carefully opened the briefcase, making sure to turn it slightly so the contents were in Doug's view. Laying inside on the felt lining was a single syringe filled with a murky, fluorescent blue substance. Although contained within the tiny glass tube, the mysterious contents seemed to shimmer, creating an effervescent aura that shined dully out of the toothless mouth of the open briefcase. Blurring the hard lines of its cylindrical confinement with cold luminescence, the mysterious liquid absorbed all natural light from the room.

Even from across the room, Doug could see the strange elixor dance and swirl inside of the small narrow tube. A motion as equally hypnotic as it was terrifying. The very idea of being injected with something that reminded him of the movie *Re-Animator* made his skin crawl and bowels drop. He read about the things crazy people did every day. Nutjobs shooting people up with homemade concoctions of ammonia and mercury and terrorists releasing poison gas on crowded subways. This was clearly one of them. Doug had never seen such a thing in his life and could only guess at the man's intentions behind administering the mystery medicine. Pulling his gun out of his waistband, he stiffly aimed at the odd figure on his couch while backing up towards the door.

"Don't move, motherfucker, or I'll blow your ugly head off!" Doug yelled, trying to sound tough instead of scared shitless.

Having almost no physical reaction to a loaded weapon being pointed at his head, the man smiled a thin, crusty smile. "Now now, must we do this song and dance every time we meet? Sit down so I can get the presentation over with. It will only take a couple minutes of your time. Just a formality on my end." Sounding annoyed and partially embarrassed for Doug, the man gestured to the worn recliner on his left. At the same time, his other hand slithered into the breast pocket of his coat.

Instantly alarmed, Doug broke from his momentary stasis and screamed, "Put your fucking hands up!" Acting purely on instinctual fear, he whipped the .38 from his waistband. Leveling the barrel, he didn't hesitate to squeeze off a shot at the dense, ashy center of the suited thing on his couch. Despite the gun going off with a thunderous *BOOM!*, the man didn't even flinch. Instead, the bullet seemed to pass right through him as if he were made completely out of dyed tissue paper. Doug knew he hit the guy—the distance between them couldn't have been more than fifteen feet—but his dusty old suit was completely untouched by blood or bullet holes. Only adding to the perplexity, the man's demeanor became one of growing impatience—not of rightful fear or searing pain. With the smoking barrel still pointed at the man's frail chest, Doug froze—a slack-jawed expression of disbelief plastered on his pale face.

"Don't worry; I'm not going to hurt you. Now come sit down and stop acting like such an imbecile." Once again, the man moodily gestured to the chair while reaching into his coat pocket.

Having either the option to run or comply with his new guest's demands, Doug reluctantly chose to comply. Cautiously, he moved back over to his chair and sat down— all the while never taking his eyes or gun off of that oddly stretched face, with its disproportioned nasal cavities and over-inflated, bloodshot eyes. Doug knew the risk he was taking by playing along with the man's game, but what's it to a man who was about to commit suicide not even five minutes ago? *If anything,* Doug smugly realized, *this clown is in much more danger than I am. He should be the one who's afraid, not me.* Truly, Doug was a broken slate with nothing left to lose. For once, his perpetually pathetic state was playing in his favor. Given the current situation, Doug was the one in control now. Not his unexpected visitor.

As long as he could keep a reasonable distance between himself and the crazy frog man with the syringe, Doug felt he could stay on top. In his fear-addled mind, the man was clearly a trained assassin of some kind. Possibly someone hired by the one of the debt agencies to scare him into paying his bills using tricks learned at Cirque du Soleil. Doug knew that as long as he had his gun, he would be safe.

But, none of that accounted for the magic bullet trick he saw just moments prior. He didn't know any form of Brazilian Jiu Jitsu that could stop a lead bullet from fifteen feet away. More than likely, some of the bullets he got with the gun were old duds—firing off as just noisy blanks. Hopefully not all three, but the chances were still in Doug's favor. Besides, he only really needed one to get the job done.

Leveling his staggered breath, Doug smoothed out his wiry nerves and boldly said, "Look, you better be trying to sell me some sort of flu shot because if this is a drug deal or some sort of extortion scheme, then just save your speech. I'm not having it." Still sitting, he slowly leaned towards the couch and sternly added, "Now…get the fuck out of my house." Doug was trying his hardest to channel Stallone or Mel Gibson, anybody tougher than his normal self. Straddling the edge of his seat, gun set and ready on the padded arm, he waited for the man to reply—ready to fire again if he even so much as flinched the wrong way. One wrong move, and Doug fully intended to shoot him directly in the face and/or dick.

Casually, the man retracted his hand from his breast pocket and set the small object down in front of the suitcase. From where Doug sat, it appeared to be a normal, run-of-the-mill, yellow onion.

Sensing Doug's immediate confusion, the man offered him another peeled smile. "I find that using a visual prop helps explain the more difficult parts. Bear with me here." Pinching the onion between his thumb and forefinger, he held it up. With his other hand, he pointed one rigid Nosferatu finger and slowly dragged it across the diameter of the onion. As if cut by an invisible Ginsu knife, the onion magically separated in two with a wet *POP!* The half not pinched in his ghoulish hand tumbled to the floor, coming to rest by Doug's chair. Still holding up the exposed half, the man began his speech.

"Every human, animal, and plant has an inherent ability to subconsciously interpret the reality or space in which they currently inhabit. The ability to distinguish a chair from a horse or a tree from an atom bomb explosion is so incredibly ordinary to you humans that most of you take the gift for granted. Ordinarily, most organic lifeforms throughout the cosmos carry an infinite number of realities or mindsets within one body or conscious entity. Much like a single onion has many layers to make one whole, beings with any form of consciousness have endless realities co-existing on a single timeline where all scenarios, no matter how mundane, play out in unison.

"In some versions of your life, Doug, you have eight kids," the man went on casually as the webbed fingers of his free hand smoothed out fine particles of clinging dust on his pants, "and in others you never get married at all. In one mindset, you are a billionaire oil tycoon with two mansions and a supermodel wife, and in others you are...well, you know." His ink dot pupils met Doug's, eyeballs rippling like two veiny Jell-O molds. Heart painfully halted in his chest, the dark energy from the man's stare quickly hollowed Doug's former sense of security.

Once again, he had foolishly gotten himself in way over his head.

"I know it's hard to grasp the idea of multiple interwoven realities, but it's true. Reality is not a shared experience, as most of your kind believes, but a subjective projection of the inner curves and lines that make up the visible universe. Humans will never fully evolve enough to experience the true unveiling of what molds and shapes life, but the onion presentation is pretty close. We are having this conversation here and now, but we are also having it in an infinite number of subdimensions. Does any of this make sense to you?"

No longer needing his visual prop, the man tossed the onion disinterestedly over his left shoulder.

"With every subjective projection comes a string of concentrated energy. Again, think of a field full of onions, each one loosely interconnected through tiny roots and microscopic fibers traveling under the soil. You can't see them from where you stand, but they are there. Those onions have an instinctual desire to reach out through the dense earth to find one another and share a reality together. One Vision, One Truth." From the man's raised fist, one scaly finger shot up in the air. He held it out to Doug, making sure his point was understood. Confused and afraid, Doug in turn said nothing and continued to passively listen—the barrel of the .38 slowly drooping towards the floor.

"This string, or root, connects to other projections, creating a tapestry of invisible threads that make up the gray areas where your people theorize dark matter originates from. When these strings are at risk of being damaged through outside means, it is my noble duty to come in and make sure that nothing is irreparably broken. Your case, though, is a special one, Doug. In almost every one of your mindsets, you either kill yourself in this room or avoid me for years until eventually I find your bloated corpse in a shallow canal or cheap motel by the interstate. No matter how many of your mindsets I visit, you always act irrationally and mutilate yourself. Quite sad, really."

The man halfheartedly chuckled to himself about this in tiny, chirping whimpers. The eerie sound reminded Doug of the nocturnal gibbering of bats—smooshed faces grimacing and wet. The chirping progressed in loudness until the man suddenly chomped down on his own tongue to stop himself. With black crude oil dribbling from the corners of his frowning mouth, the man continued his lengthy sales pitch.

"It's crazy, but in some mindsets you don't even own a gun. Sometimes, when I approach your door and try to give you this talk just as I am now, you simply grab the closest object and off yourself with it. Oh! One time I watched you smash that portrait over there, shattering the glass pane, and then practically sever your own wrists with the shards. And on another occasion, you stabbed yourself in the jugular with an open pair of scissors. Sometimes I can almost get you to comply, and other times I knock on the door just as you turn your brains into a fine mist on that back wall."

The man awkwardly paused while his head jerked roughly to one side, a violent glitch in the simulation. Nervously, Doug glanced over at the photo lined wall. He could barely make out all the family photos, ones capturing better times in his life, as his head swelled with a cocktail of madness and enlightenment. Too scared to cry, his eyeballs swelled with bottled tears for everything he had lost. Doug didn't know it yet, but with the fate of an entire conscious tapestry resting on his head, he had once again established worth.

For once in his miserable life, he had control.

"Sure, there are mindsets where you live a perfectly normal life and never hurt yourself, but those are buried under the incomprehensible amount of times that you *do* disturb the balance, thus canceling them out entirely. It is truly odd to see one particular reality where the outcome is almost always the same. It's anomalies like this that make even *me* wonder if there is more to the Divinity. This endless waterfall of pointless, unrelenting awareness to one's own lack of control over what we perceive as destiny…it's just nuts."

While the man seemed to be contemplating the irony of this statement, Doug took the opportunity to speak.

"I don't know whether you're high or just insane, but I want this to stop now. This is the last time I'm going to tell you to get the fuck out of my house. You can't just walk up in here and spread a bunch of horseshit about parallel universes and invisible strings and whatnot. What do you want me to believe, that you're an alien or some kind of time traveler, or some other dumb shit like that? Get real."

The man took a moment to quietly contemplate, clucking his tongue exactly eight times between thoughts. Finally, he calmly retorted, "No, Doug, I'm not an alien. I exist in all realms simultaneously while occupying one form. It's exactly what you do subconsciously, except I can navigate and control when and where I am going and who I'm going in. Think of me as a god, minus the forced worshiping and boring book series. As for *alien*, while being capable of interdimensional travel, most do not have the evolutionary capabilities needed for vast omnipotent viewing. I don't simply travel in time; I become a part of it. By simultaneously being on the outside and inside of the linear framework—like a fisherman with his pole cast and feet submerged into an isolated body of flowing water—I am free of dimensional barricades and cornered realms."

Dead air filled the empty spaces where harsh silence now blanketed the entire living room. Doug's lower back ached annoyingly at his refusal to ease into the soft padding of his chair. *I wonder if this is what doing DMT feels like?* Doug distantly wondered. *Except...I know this isn't a hallucination...this is real. And if I don't want this asshole putting me under so he can steal both my kidneys for re-sale, I need to start thinking straight...*

The man folded his leather raked fingers into one another; two hairless tarantulas gnawing at the other's belly. A whistling breath rushed out the man's flared pencil hole nostrils as he said, "I am here because you are a defective consciousness, Doug. And if I let you carry on this self-destructive pattern, you will eventually cause a ripple effect, sending negative impulses and energy to countless other healthy mindsets. In this syringe is the solution to all your problems—to everyone's problems. The only way to ensure that this escalating disobedience to the grand chaos of reality isn't further disturbed. Now, while I am not permitted to physically administer the shot, I can assist you in transitioning over to the Otherside. Free of charge."

Doug sat for almost a full minute, steeped in concentrated thought, before harshly whispering, "So, let me get this straight. You want me to mainline that blue shit so I can die and stop the timeline crisis, is that right? There's only one problem with your cute lil story, bub; I was already one step ahead of you. If you wanted me dead so badly, you should've just waited fifteen fuckin' minutes and let my .38 do the job—"

Without warning, the man slammed a bony fist onto the coffee table, sending a shower of wood dust and splinters. Hand still curled into a fist, he punched a hole clean through the tabletop while somehow not damaging its structural integrity. Beady eyes enflamed with rage, he slowly turned to Doug and snarled, "NOOO!" so loudly it rattled the surrounding windowpanes. "Open your ears and listen to me! This shot will not kill you—it will force you to evolve consciously to a higher state of being! It is the only way to ensure the end of your timeline! Stupid monkey!"

Seeing the strange man's angry desperation suddenly cleared the mental fog from Doug's mind. Confident for the first time in ages, he sat up straight and confrontationally asked, "What do you have to gain from all this, guy? What's in it for you if I take the shot? Yeah, I heard the whole part about me infecting other timelines or whatever, but if you exist outside of all this, then what's the big fuckin' deal? Why not simply look the other way and let me keep up the pattern? In theory, if there are an infinite number of mindsets and outcomes like you say, then eventually this whole situation will solve itself. Right? If it is what it is, then why waste your breath on—"

Suddenly, the man momentarily disappeared only to re-materialize in Doug's lap. Pinned back in his chair by cold, slimy talons, Doug reflexively fought back against the vice. But no matter how much he thrashed and bucked to break free of the man's impossibly tight grip, the substantial weight remained. The man's face—now a stone wall of cracked lunacy—leered down at him. Perched atop his chest like a giant pigeon, the man stared right through Doug's soul with eyes so black that Doug could see his own terrified expression mirrored back at him. The empty slots of the man's eyes—swimming in the sooty complexion of his ashy skin—were nothing but jet-black disks that seemed to hold eternity. The swirling black mass instantly filled Doug with dread so rotten and pure that he hardly noticed emptying his bowels. Like the deadly syringe, the disks had that dull glow that seemed to envelop and waver in the space between them. As if the air molecules were being replaced with a new and much superior element, Doug found it increasingly harder to breathe as the man leaned in closer.

"You will do as I say, peasant!" he screeched down at Doug. "DO AS I SAAAY!"

With one elastic arm, the man reached across the room while keeping his perched position on top of Doug. Dipping into the open briefcase, he snatched up the syringe and retracted his arm with one awkward jerk as if his appendage were nothing more than a kinked-up measuring tape dispenser. Menacingly, he then commenced to dangle the cold cylinder directly in front of Doug's terror-stricken face. The precious liquid lazily sloshed back and forth inside the syringe as the man swayed it in a hypnotically pendulous motion.

"Either you inject this into yourself now, or I'm going to eat your face!" the man squealed not twelve inches away from Doug's face. "Then...I'll rip off your wife's tits and castrate your children! How's that sound?!"

Chapped lips stretched thin over his exposed mouth of rusty teeth—eyes practically leaking out onto his crusty cheeks—the man heaved and thrashed in Doug's lap like a spastic child throwing a tantrum. Comatose with fear, Doug sat with both hands tucked into the sides of his chair, not wanting to touch the foul thing that wriggled and cried in his lap.

Suddenly, he remembered his trusty pistol.

In his initial panic, it had slid to the floor when the man teleported into his chair. To the best of his knowledge, it probably landed by the onion half at his right side. With only one alternative left, he felt along the floor with his foot and found the gun with ease. He made a mental note of where it had landed but did not let the fundamental discovery show on his pale face.

Forcing the last bit of moisture to his impossibly dry mouth, Doug reluctantly mumbled, "Okay…give me the needle. I'll do it. Just promise me that you won't hurt Maggie or the boys."

At this, the strange man screeched in utter joy while his cracked hands palpated rapidly against each other in a series of spastic golf claps. Slithering roughly off Doug's lap, he proceeded to bounce his rubbery body to the middle of the room—eyes ping-ponging around in their sockets like drunken crickets. Loudly, he rejoiced in an almost certain victory. "Yesyesyes! I'm so glad you finally came to your senses, Doug!"

As the man's celebration petered, he turned back and faced Doug's chair—greedy smile stretched ear to ear. But as he did, that smile quickly faded; Doug was now holding the .38. While the man was distracted, he had snatched the gun off the floor, and now had it placed firmly to his temple. Caught off guard by his display of naked hubris, the man stood frozen in surprise, knowing all too well that he just squashed the whole deal.

Again.

"Well, well," Doug proudly sneered, index finger looped hard around the hair trigger, "will you still want to eat my face after I put a big smoking crater in it? Hm? Looks to me like your bluff didn't go over as well as you wanted it to. I will admit that you had me going for a while there, but I eventually figured out your little lie. While the part about

207

you being omnipotent and of a higher evolutionary species is probably true, the very notion that you are god-like is utter bullshit. I may be a loser, but I know a hack when I see one. Why would a god run around after the likes of me throughout eternity? Why not just cast your will down upon me then and there? Or, even better, prevent my birth from ever even happening so there are no corrupted mindsets to later endanger the fabric of reality? If I had to guess, I'd say you either owe someone a huge debt, or are simply a slave to some cruel master that has sentenced you to this meager existence."

Holding his arm steady, he eagerly added, "If I had to guess, I'd say your purpose is to relive this moment until I either take the shot or you die. If you're even capable of dying, that is. The way I see it, you're already living in the literal definition of Hell, so I don't know if death is something you'd even look forward to at this point."

Breaking from his speech, Doug softly chuckled to himself before adding, "It's funny; here I was, pitying myself and hating life, when all along my life has been pretty great. Up until this morning, I thought I had no purpose, but I was just too dumb and greedy to see the truth until just now."

With a twitchy grin, Doug humbly nodded. "And for that…I thank you, sir."

Before the man could retort, the loaded .38 responded with a deafening *BOOM!*

Game. Set. Match.

"Time's up," Doug murmured to himself, his voice gently reverberating off the corners of the now vacant living room. "Time to go to Heaven and tap-dance with Jesus."

Slowly, he stood up from his chair and approached the fireplace mantel. Reaching up, he then took down the loaded crossbow hanging on the wall and firmly placed it under his chin.

But, as his curled finger battled the loaded pressure of the trigger, a series of frantic knocks rattled at the front door...

SKIPPY

Mom and Dad were always pretty strict about what my sister and I watched for television growing up. While Dad was mostly in control of the remote, I'm pretty sure Mom was the little man behind the curtain when it came to what was considered wholesome entertainment for us young and impressionable kids.

For Dad, it was either daytime game shows or the news. Anything else to him was, and I quote, "jumped up trash," or "mindless fluff."

"You see, Jeffery, game shows teach you the value of things," he'd always rant, "the worth of commerce. The news? Mah! The news gives you the skippy on everything else. An', at the end of the day, all's that's left is the skippy."

He always made sure to end with that annoying word whenever he gave that tired old anecdote—which back then was often. I'm sure it was supposed to mean something to him, but even now I still can't figure out exactly what that might be.

Parental locks were in place on all but two channels.

The only kids' show we were allowed to watch was Mr. Roger's Neighborhood, but the puppets on the other side of the wall scared me too much. It was something about the way they moved—plastic faces pinched and nubbed arms restlessly twitching. As for movies, Dad only took me out one time. It was to see an afternoon reshowing of *Patton*— said I needed to see what real men used to look like. I dozed off halfway through the long speech at the beginning. Real men were boring back then.

By six, I was culturally retarded to what most of the other kids were watching. There were so many cartoons and movies I missed out on that even if I lived for two full lifetimes, I'd never be able to catch up. But I couldn't let the others know that. In a desperate bid to fit in, I learned everything I could secondhand—off the cuff, on the playground, between classes. When someone was chatting at the swing set about the newest Star Wars movie or KISS record, I'd soak it up and save —regurgitate later. I'd latch onto key words and phrases. Anything I could slide into conversation to seem normal. But only if pressed to. I knew if I got too cocky and mouthed off like one of them, I'd expose myself.

For a couple years, I stayed away from TV completely. I found more comfort in being alone, sleeping or playing in the woods. There was lots of cool stuff out there for anyone who bothered to look. But, it wasn't long until I got bored with the same old same old. Poking through empty gopher holes and fermented squirrel guts had its limits.

One rainy day while Dad was at work, Mom was napping, and Jade was playing with her dolls down the hall in the nursery, I decided to try again. I made sure the living room was completely empty before I left the couch. Breathless, I crossed the room on glass legs and stood before the giant oak-framed television.

Flipping the on/off switch, the hidden tubes flickered with a soft *plink*, followed by a hot sizzle of sound. Immediately, a grey and white dot of fuzz widened and sharpened into scratched lines of wooly color across the scuffed glass. Quickly turning the volume down to a metallic whisper, I sat cross-legged on the floor in front of the screen. Dad locked up the remote during the day, so I had to use the wobbly dials on the front panel.

When the picture finally focused, it showed a young couple; man and woman, bronzed by the sun, walking along the beach, both smiling and holding hands. Scratchy violins hummed quietly in the background of this hawk-like view— barely audible over the swelling static of crashing waves. As the camera slowly panned in from across the sand, the couple continued to walk along the foaming rim of darkened beach, talking and laughing in a silent tongue. As the box closes in on them you can see the tapered end of a burning cigarette hanging from both of their phony actor smiles. I flipped the station just as the man leaned in dramatically to kiss the girl, blowing a lung full of velvety black smoke into her Botox puckered mouth.

But before their lips could touch, the screen went totally blank. A new channel slowly funneled in.

This new picture showed a dark set of woods; dimly lit, tiny faucets of twinkling starlight. The wordless chatter of dry branches rubbing together in the nightly breeze faded in and out of the tiny speaker. Suddenly, two disjointed eyes of light poked through the swaying net of trees, followed by the distant sound of crunching footsteps. The shot held. The lights got bigger—footsteps louder. The wide shot finally broke to the source of the lights; two shadowy figures trudging through the woods. Their features hidden under the looming veil of night. Balanced, the camera kept a steady pace with them just a few feet away.

Interested, I turned up the volume knob another notch and leaned into the screen to cut the glare from the curtained windows. As I concentrated, the soft tapping of rain receded from the whirling wind to reveal the strained voices of the two figures.

"Jesusjesusjesus, did you see that?! Ahfuckjesus, man…" I heard one shape whisper to the other, an infliction of naked fear seeping through. Kinda angry, kinda scared. The figure walking ahead either didn't hear or was ignoring the other. His quick stride through the trees never lessened. Regardless, the scared shape followed.

"Hey!" the follower finally barked, refusing to trudge any farther. The whole screen was now her face hanging over the beam of a flashlight. A girl.

She was young—not as young as me, but definitely not as old as Dad or Mom. I wasn't good with celebrities, but this girl didn't look like one. She was pretty enough, but something about her red eyes, flushed skin, and runny make-up was unusual. Too real and imperfect for the screen. Rogue strands of gold-spun hair gleaming with sweat, her red button nose and wide lips reminded me of no one I'd ever seen before. Most chilling of all, her eyes wildly bulged as she spoke—two hardboiled eggs cooking in the pressure cooker of her skull.

The figure ahead, now actively listening, stopped but did not turn around to face her.

The scared girl moved forward. "You said this was gonna be easy! No one would notice, remember?! Well, the fuck happened back there!?" Her voice rose sharply to a shrill scream. The tail end of her question bounced off into the sleeping hills and caves beyond frame.

The picture quickly cut back to the figure standing with its back to frame. It didn't move or speak. Clothes damp in the peripheral dim of their flashlights, it waited.

"Say something! You crazy fuck!" the scared girl yelled, no longer able to contain herself. "You told me this shit wouldn't happen! You promised, Jeffery!"

It was only then that the silent stranger turned to face us.

Not hearing my own name at first, I stared dead on at

215

the silent canvas of the man's face until suddenly—*CLICK*. I knew this man—but I didn't. I didn't know anybody older except Mom and Dad. Another hard *CLICK* halted my blood and turned my heart cold. I realized that the same empty stare, the one I saw in the mirror every single day when I brushed my teeth, was the same as his. The rest of the face was different; sunken and shallow, grey with despair. But there was no denying it now. I don't know how—or why—but I was looking at an older version of myself on television.

I adamantly fought the idea until the man spoke, his voice deeper and stripped of its innocence, but undeniably mine.

"It's here. I know it is. Just shut up and follow me."

That's when the girl's flashlight swept over his body—revealing clothes stained brown with drying blood.

Terrified, I reflexively punched the on/off switch. The screen reversed its picture back to a fuzzy dot. Then nothing.

After telling myself there was no way I could be on TV, 20 years older, running through the woods covered in blood, I calmed down a little. It couldn't be me—just couldn't. There was no conceivable way...was there? Having to prove the whole crazy notion was all in my head, I reached out and hit the power switch again.

When the screen blew up with color, the girl and her bloody friend were gone. Replaced by an elderly couple walking along the beach. They looked a little like the couple from the first commercial, except much, much older. Their stride achingly slow, bodies bent in half against the slicing ocean wind, they walked hand in hand. As before, the shot closed in from far away on their faces, combing the sand with pruned age. From each of their spit crusted mouths dangled a length of clear tubing. A fresh cigarette plugged the wrinkled holes in their throats. Wrinkled hands pulled the burning cigs away to expose frothy, puss-crusted pits dripping with blue smoke—toothless second mouths gumming and hacking. The yawning gashes coughed and frowned to the camera, spitting up thick bubbles of greenish slobber like eyeless newborns. Staining the clean white filters of their cigarettes the same filthy color of city rain water, the loose phlegm steadily leaked from the holes in a slow trickle. The whole thing was so disgusting, so incredibly vile, but the camera kept pulling in.

Closer.

Closer.

Closer.

The picture got clearer, the holes kept growing.

But, before my eyes could slide inside, I flailed my arms out and flipped the switch back off.

Blankness returned to the screen. To the world.

My reflection, shrunken and pale in the smooth glass curvature, receded back into the depths of the black cube.

And as I watched myself disappear, my Dad's phantom voice echoed out between us,

"...all's that's left is the skippy... is the skippy... the skippy... skippy..."